"I honestly feel ba̶̶̶̶̶̶̶̶̶̶̶̶̶̶̶̶r. Burnham declared. "I̶̶̶̶̶̶̶̶̶̶̶̶̶̶̶̶m imposing upon your holiday. But it's only a small mission." His light blue eyes were filled with concern as his gaze met mine.

"What is it?" I asked gently.

"I was only wondering if you'd look in on my London house once or twice while you're there."

"Is that all?" I asked, surprised. "But why does your house need checking?"

"Because my live-in housekeeper, Mrs. Elliott, isn't answering the phone. I've been calling for the past five days, and I'm worried she may be ill. She's rather elderly, I'm afraid. Maybe something happened to her."

The waiter brought our lunches, and I took a few minutes to eat and ponder Dr. Burnham's request. I mean, I was happy to take the time to check his house, but why couldn't he ask a friend to look in for him?

NANCY DREW
girl detective™

#1 Without a Trace

#2 A Race Against Time

#3 False Notes

#4 High Risk

#5 Lights, Camera . . .

#6 Action!

#7 The Stolen Relic

#8 The Scarlet Macaw Scandal

#9   Secret of the Spa

#10 Uncivil Acts

#11 Riverboat Ruse

#12 Stop the Clock

#13 Trade Wind Danger

#14 Bad Times, Big Crimes

#15 Framed

#16 Dangerous Plays

Available from Aladdin Paperbacks

NANCY DREW

DREW

girl detective ™

#16

Dangerous Plays

CAROLYN KEENE

Aladdin Paperbacks

New York   London   Toronto   Sydney

This book is a work of fiction. Any references to historical events, real people, or real locales are used fictitiously. Other names, characters, places, and incidents are the product of the author's imagination, and any resemblance to actual events or locales or persons, living or dead, is entirely coincidental.

❧ ALADDIN PAPERBACKS
An imprint of Simon & Schuster Children's Publishing Division
1230 Avenue of the Americas, New York, NY 10020
Copyright © 2006 by Simon & Schuster, Inc.
All rights reserved, including the right of
reproduction in whole or in part in any form.
NANCY DREW is a registered trademark of Simon & Schuster, Inc.
ALADDIN PAPERBACKS, NANCY DREW: GIRL DETECTIVE, and
colophon are trademarks of Simon & Schuster, Inc.
Manufactured in the United States of America
First Aladdin Paperbacks edition March 2006
10 9 8 7 6 5 4
Library of Congress Control Number 2005936496
ISBN-13: 978-1-4169-0605-6
ISBN-10: 1-4169-0605-3

Contents

1	*Words of Warning*	1
2	*Rude Strangers*	12
3	*Crime Scene*	22
4	*Kidnapped!*	30
5	*A Mysterious Blonde*	36
6	*Ghost Stories*	49
7	*Danger at the Top*	60
8	*Don't Mess with Tea*	67
9	*Clued Out*	78
10	*Locked In*	87
11	*Upstaged*	103
12	*Showdown*	116
13	*A Moonlit Stalker*	124
14	*A Rare Conspiracy*	131

Dangerous Plays

Words of Warning

I was in a race against time, and as of noon today, there was no telling who the winner would be.

My heart pounded with excitement as I thought about my upcoming trip. Dad, Bess Marvin, and I were heading to London, England, on the 9:00 p.m. flight! In just a few more hours, I'd be seeing Big Ben, Westminster Abbey, Buckingham Palace, and awesome theater. What more could I want? And with my wonderful dad and my best friend along to share the sights, I considered myself an extremely lucky girl. That was the good news. Now for the bad. I was staring at an empty suitcase, and we were leaving for the airport in five hours. And I still had to get to the bank!

Clothes flew out of my closet and dresser drawers as I dug frantically through my stuff, deciding on what I would take. My favorite green T-shirt, blue jeans, a peach-colored tank—all fought for airspace on their way to the open suitcase on my bed. With any luck, maybe a T-shirt or two would actually land in it.

The phone rang. I groaned. Why did I have to leave all the boring stuff like packing till the last minute? No way did I have time for chitchat now. I resisted the temptation to answer it.

The ringing stopped, and a moment later Hannah Gruen, our housekeeper, called me from downstairs. Hannah has been like a mother to me since my own mom died when I was three. As usual, my heart warmed to the sound of her voice. "Nancy! It's Ned. He says it is really important."

Ned Nickerson is my boyfriend. Unfortunately, he was studying for a Shakespeare exam, so he couldn't come to London with us. A week without Ned was the only downside of the trip, so I thanked Hannah and picked up the phone beside my bed. I mean, one last good-bye wouldn't set my schedule back too much, would it? I promised myself I'd be quick.

"Hey, Ned! What's up? Hannah said it's something important."

Ned's low voice came through the receiver. "I'm

really sorry to bother you, Nancy, but my Shakespeare professor, Dr. Burnham, wants to meet you for lunch."

"Now?"

"He has some problem he wants to run by you. He says it can't wait. Something to do with his house in London. I told him you're going over there, and I guess I must have mentioned you're a detective. Sorry about that."

"Detective?" I perked up at the word. "Don't be sorry, Ned. You couldn't know that his problem would be so pressing. Plus, you know me too well—I can't resist a mystery, if that's what this is. Anyway, I would have been disappointed if you hadn't called."

Ned laughed. "I thought you'd say something like that."

I hesitated, looking at the mess in my room. "Still, I don't see how I can possibly meet him. Dad wants to leave right at five o'clock, and you know what a stickler for time he is." As the most successful lawyer in our hometown of River Heights, Dad is incredibly organized. He has to be. That's how he wins his cases, by paying close attention to detail and staying one step ahead of everyone else. Leaving for the airport at a minute past five would be sloppy and, worse, risky. I couldn't do that to him.

"I promise it'll be a quick lunch," Ned assured me.

"We can meet at the Moonbeam Diner on Bluff Street near your house. You'll need to eat anyway. Did I mention that I'll be there too?"

How could I refuse him? Against my better judgment, I heard myself agreeing to meet them in half an hour at the diner. I'd just have to let my packing slide. I mean, what's a forgotten pair of shoes compared to a brand-new case?

Mysteries are my passion. And even though I'm still pretty young, I've solved many cases that stumped our local police force. No matter where I am, mysteries seem to follow me around like a pack of faithful dogs. And why not? I love them, I pay them lots of attention, and so they're always hounding me. So much for taking a break from detective work by escaping to London.

Promptly at twelve thirty, I arrived at the Moonbeam Diner and found an empty booth. After ordering a chocolate milkshake and a burger, I waited for the rest of my party. Soon I saw Ned's tall figure come through the door, followed by a handsome man of medium height with chestnut brown hair, black-rimmed glasses, and a shy demeanor. I judged him to be in his midthirties. Dr. Burnham, I presumed.

Ned's face lit up when he saw me. "Hey, Nancy!" he said, sliding into the seat beside me while Dr. Burnham sat down across the table. "Thanks so much for meeting us. I'll take full responsibility with your dad if you're not ready by five." He grinned, pushing back a stray lock of brown hair. "Meanwhile, I'd like you to meet my Shakespeare professor, Dr. Samuel Burnham."

I extended my hand. "Hi, I'm Nancy Drew. It's nice to meet you, Dr. Burnham."

"Likewise, Nancy," Dr. Burnham said in a British accent as we shook hands. "I understand you're heading across the pond tonight. At least, that's what Ned mentioned earlier today." He dropped his gaze for a moment before looking at me tentatively once more.

"My father is taking my friend Bess and me to London for a week. I can't wait. We've been wanting to see some plays at the Globe Theatre, and he finally got a break in his busy schedule. And since Bess has been studying Shakespeare's comedies in a night class, Dad and I wanted to invite her, too."

"Well, you couldn't see Shakespeare in a better place than the Globe Theatre," Dr. Burnham said. "It's a replica of Shakespeare's original theater from four hundred years ago when he wrote his plays. The architects tried to recreate everything as faithfully as possible, down to the wooden benches and the thatched roof. It's even on the original site." He went on to explain more about the Globe and about Shakespeare's life and times.

"Were you teaching in London before you came to River Heights?" I asked.

"I'm on exchange this semester from the University of London," he explained. "I've been teaching Shakespeare there for several years. In my spare time, though, I'm a playwright. I'm equally passionate about teaching Shakespeare and writing my own work, but, of course, I wouldn't presume to mention the Bard's plays in the same breath as my own," he added modestly.

"Maybe you could give me some tips on Shakespeare for our trip," I told him.

"I'm sure your friend Bess will be perfectly knowledgeable," Dr. Burnham said. "After all, she's taking her night course."

"So George is out of luck on this trip just because she's slacking off in the evenings?" Ned asked me, a teasing glint in his warm brown eyes. George Fayne was my other best friend and Bess's cousin. Ned knew that I'd never leave George out of anything that included Bess. My friends are incredibly important to me. No way would I choose one and not the other.

I smiled. "We invited her, but she turned us down. She's running in a marathon next week. Kind of like you and your Shakespeare exam—an unfortunate scheduling conflict."

Dr. Burnham threw Ned an apologetic look as I continued, "Even Hannah has an excuse to stay home. She wants to garden and supervise house repairs. I can't believe you guys all said no to London."

Ned shrugged. "Hannah is probably looking forward to a relaxing week of peace and quiet. Being a tourist can get stressful. All that running around to historic sites and listening to tour guides drone on when your feet hurt."

Dr. Burnham laughed, but then quickly turned solemn. "I'm afraid I'm about to add to your stress, Nancy. Did Ned tell you why I wanted to see you?"

"He mentioned something to do with your house," I replied, pushing my shoulder-length reddish blond hair behind my ears. "But he wasn't specific."

"I honestly feel bad about asking you this," Dr. Burnham declared. "I hope you won't think I'm imposing upon your holiday. But it's only a small mission." His light blue eyes were filled with concern as his gaze met mine. I knew he hoped I'd agree to help him, but he seemed timid about demanding a favor for fear I'd be inconvenienced.

"What is it?" I asked gently.

"I was only wondering if you'd look in on my London house once or twice while you're there."

"Is that all?" I asked, surprised. "But why does your house need checking?"

"Because my live-in housekeeper, Mrs. Elliott, isn't answering the phone. I've been calling for the past five days, and I'm worried she may be ill. She's rather elderly, I'm afraid. Maybe something happened to her."

The waiter brought our lunches, and I took a few minutes to eat and ponder Dr. Burnham's request. I mean, I was happy to take the time to check his house, but why couldn't he ask a friend to look in for him?

"And that's not all," Dr. Burnham continued, breaking into my thoughts. "Before I left for the U.S. at the end of January, there were some odd things going on in my house. Very subtle but definitely not my imagination."

"Odd things?" I echoed. "Like what?"

"Oh, nothing big. Stuff like pictures askew on the wall when I'd come down to breakfast in the morning. Footsteps creaking downstairs in the middle of the night. My stash of tea strangely depleted. And Mrs. Elliott noticed these things too. And none of those occurrences would be that remarkable if Mrs. Elliott hadn't suddenly vanished overnight."

Privately, I thought the word "vanished" was a bit overblown, but I listened respectfully as he added,

"I'm very concerned about her—and my house."

"Do you know any of her family or friends?" Ned asked. "Could you call them?"

"I believe she has an estranged husband," Dr. Burnham replied. "Of course I'll track him down, if worse comes to worse. But, Nancy, if you wouldn't mind just dropping by and giving the house a quick look, I'd be most grateful to you." He fished in the pocket of his tweed jacket and pulled out a copy of an old-fashioned skeleton key. "Here's an extra key, just in case you find a moment." He pushed it across the table.

Studying him, I felt a wave of disappointment. Mrs. Elliott was probably just taking a few days off and had forgotten to tell him. The strange noises in his house at night most likely had a simple four-legged explanation—mice. Or maybe a two-legged one—Mrs. Elliott sleepwalking. Or else Dr. Burnham had been guzzling more tea than usual. Whatever. Anyway, this obviously wasn't the mystery I'd been hoping for.

"Why don't you ask a friend to check your house for you? I mean, since you say that finding Mr. Elliott might get complicated."

Dr. Burnham sighed. "I already asked a colleague of mine at the university to do just that. But since Mrs. Elliott and I are the only people who have keys, his visit was rather useless. He knocked on the door, but unfortunately, the house was as silent as a tomb. Then he looked through some windows and found nothing the least bit wrong. That's why I made this spare key for you."

The shiny silver key gleamed up at me from the table. It reminded my of the key that Alice had needed to open the door to Wonderland—the key that always seemed to stay out of her reach. I glanced again at Dr. Burnham's hopeful gaze. Maybe I should just grab this key while I had the chance. So what if it didn't lead to anything as interesting as Wonderland? At least I'd be doing Ned's professor a favor, which would basically be doing Ned a favor. I placed the key in my pocket, sealing the deal.

"There's something more I need to tell you, Nancy," Dr. Burnham added. "Something rather ominous."

More ominous than disappearing tea? "I'm on the edge of my seat," I assured him.

Rummaging once more in his pocket, he drew out a letter and handed it to me. It was postmarked London five days ago and sent to Dr. Burnham at his River Heights address near the college campus. "This friendly little greeting arrived in yesterday's mail. Please, Nancy, have a look. I think you'll understand that this job is way too complex for an amateur like my professor friend. It requires an experienced detective, like you."

I unfolded a piece of powder blue stationery and stared at a note handwritten in black fountain pen. The message was a warning, brief and to the point: *Your house is next on our list!*

2

Rude Strangers

There's no return address," I observed as I turned the envelope around, looking for clues.

Dr. Burnham frowned as I handed the letter back to him. "Nancy, do you see now why I want an actual sleuth to check out my house? My professor friend, while quite well-meaning, would be useless. This message has made me very concerned. Now if Mrs. Elliott would only answer the phone, I'd feel better, but I must confess I barely slept last night after receiving this letter. So when Ned mentioned that his girlfriend, who is a detective, was on her way to London, I simply had to meet with you."

I checked my watch: 1:30 p.m. The bank was still on my To Do list—and also the bookstore, I just remembered. Traveler's checks and a London guidebook were just as important to me as clothes. I was going to have to cut this meeting short. Sure, I sympathized with Dr. Burnham, but sympathy wouldn't help either of us if I missed my plane. Still, I had a couple more questions.

"Have you told the police about the note?" I asked.

"I've been tempted to call them, but since nothing bad has happened yet, what would I say to them? The police are frightfully busy, Nancy, and problems like crooked pictures probably wouldn't impress them. I'm more comfortable using a private detective like you."

Ned signaled the waiter for the check, while Dr. Burnham added, "I hope you won't mind checking my house, Nancy. Morning, noon, and night, I've thought about nothing else. I haven't been able to concentrate on any of my work—not my teaching, not my writing. I inherited that house from my parents, and it has all the possessions I care about in the world inside it, including two rare books that are the most precious things I own." His voice, normally soft and mild, became robust, and his sky blue eyes flashed with resolve. I smiled. "I'll be happy to do what I can. Could you jot down your address and phone number for me?" I pushed my notepad toward him. Shooting me a look of grateful relief, he began to write.

"And by the way, lunch is on me," he added as he handed me back my notepad. "It's the least I can do to thank both of you. Anyway, Nancy, I hope I didn't take up too much of your time before takeoff."

"Are you kidding, Dr. Burnham?" Ned said, throwing me a sly sidelong glance. "You've just given Nancy an awesome good-bye gift—a new mystery to solve. Who knows? Maybe she'll be inspired to get to the airport early!"

The rain made soft tapping sounds against the windshield of the cab as we sped from Heathrow Airport into the city of London. "Typical London weather," Bess commented happily, "gray and drizzly. The streetlights look cool the way they glow in the fog. They're like something out of a Sherlock Holmes story."

You'd think my friend would be upset by the rain, but thoughts of wearing her new designer raincoat purchased for our trip had put her in an especially cheerful mood. But Bess usually found ways to make the best out of any circumstances. Yes, she loved clothes and cherished her creature comforts, but Bess was no pampered princess. In fact, she was one of the best sports I knew—honest, kind, and brave. She's helped me get to the bottom of mysteries many times, despite her basic dread of danger. I mean, what could be more courageous than confronting your fears for a friend?

At any rate I doubted Dr. Burnham's case would be a dangerous one. Even the so-called ominous note that he'd gotten had a fake sound to it, as if the writer had watched too many bad mystery movies. *Your house is next on our list.* What did that mean? For all anyone knew, the message could have come from a real estate agent. So I relaxed in the cab as we made our way through the rain-soaked streets to our hotel in the posh London neighborhood of Mayfair.

"Wow, Dad, you really splurged!" I exclaimed as we pulled up to a gracious building fronted by a white-pillared portico. A crimson banner with a white swan emblazoned on it flapped cheerfully in the gusty breeze, while a friendly doorman in a red coat similar to those worn by the queen's guards opened our door with a flourish.

Dad smiled. "Well, Nancy," he said as he paid the cab driver. "You know I've been working hard these past few months, and I feel bad that I haven't been around the house as much as usual. So when I won my last case, I decided to treat us to something special. The White Swan was recommended by one of my English clients, who promised a comfortable but not too flashy place."

As usual, Dad was proved right the moment we

entered the lobby. With its oriental carpet, dark wood-paneled walls, and solicitous porters, the hotel felt more like someone's elegant home than temporary housing for tourists.

"This is exactly how I imagined London, Mr. Drew," Bess said as we followed one of the porters into an old-fashioned elevator with gates and a lever. "Cozy but also fancy. In a nice way, I mean."

I knew exactly what Bess meant. Our room on the fourth floor, linked to Dad's by a door, was quiet and comfortable. The wall sconces and bronze chandelier cast a golden light on the soft carpet and canopy beds, making the rain outside seem warm and soothing.

Once we'd settled in, Dad, Bess, and I grabbed a quick lunch in the pub on the corner near our hotel. "This is called a ploughman's lunch," Dad explained as his cheese and bread arrived with a pickle on the side. "A common English snack."

Bess and I shared a caesar salad—we were too excited to be very hungry—while I took a guidebook from my backpack and searched for Dr. Burnham's address on its fold-out map. During the plane ride I'd told Bess and Dad about Dr. Burnham's mystery. Dad, as usual, had cautioned me to be careful, but Bess hadn't been impressed. "Knowing you, Nancy," she'd declared, "I'm sure you'll figure out what's going on the first day we're there." Did I mention Bess is loyal?

As I took another bite of salad, I was eager to put her confidence to the test. Pointing to a spot on the map not far from our hotel, I said, "Dr. Burnham's address is Fifty-three Banbury Square, right here. It's in a part of town called Knightsbridge."

"Then it must be near Harrods. You know, the famous London department store?" Bess said. I must have looked kind of clueless, because she quickly added, "Trust me, Nancy. Harrods is famous. I'd like to go there at some point during our trip, maybe to buy my parents and sister some presents. Harrods has everything. Clothes, jewelry, food, you name it."

I made an "okay" circle with my thumb and fore-finger, then said, "But first, let's drop by Dr. Burnham's house."

"I'll come too," Dad offered, flicking off a crumb that had dropped on his tie. I studied his warm blue eyes, which were filled with concern. I knew Dad would prefer to go back to our hotel and nap. Jet lag after such a long flight was no joke, and Dad had been slogging away on his case these past few weeks. But I could also tell he was anxious about me and Bess.

No question about it. Dad gives me lots of freedom because he trusts me to stay safe. Still, whenever he has the chance, he likes to personally make sure that nothing will hurt me. That is just the way Dad is—a protective parent, caring, but also trusting. I may be biased, but in my opinion, he's the best.

After lunch we strolled through the drizzle to 53 Banbury Square, a stately eighteenth-century white town house overlooking a small square with spreading oak trees and lush well-tended gardens. The neighborhood looked pretty fancy to me, and I could see that if Dr. Burnham hadn't inherited his house, he may not have been able to afford it on a professor's salary.

I led the way through the portico pillars and rang the front doorbell. No answer. I rang again. Still no answer. "Let me try the key," I said, taking it out of my raincoat pocket and sticking it into the keyhole. It wouldn't budge! "This key doesn't work," I announced, surprised.

"Let me try," Bess offered. Bess's love of fashion masks an awesome mechanical ability. She is as good as any car mechanic at fixing a leaky carburetor, and she's also handy at small things, like getting a key to work. But Bess didn't have any better luck than I did with this key.

"Weird!" I said, frustrated.

"Not really," Dad said. "Sometimes copies of keys don't work. That's why locksmiths always tell you to check a new copy before counting on it to open your door."

"Maybe we should come back later," Bess suggested. "Mrs. Elliott may just be out shopping."

I doubted that. I mean, if she hadn't been answering the phone for days, why would she suddenly turn up later? I bit my lip in frustration that the key didn't work. Still, what other choice did we have but to take a break and try again?

Bess had a sixth sense for Harrods, which she led us to without once consulting the map. And she was right about the store. Harrods was chock-full of everything, from the most exotic foods you could ever imagine to awesome clothes to glittery crystal to knickknacks, which Bess stocked up on for Maggie, her twelve-year-old sister. Soon we were all shopped out, so we hit the streets again, hoping we'd have better luck at Dr. Burnham's this time around.

The moment we turned the corner, I could tell things were looking up. The windows, which had been dark on our earlier visit, now poured rectangles of soft lamplight onto the rainy sidewalk. Behind lace curtains, two shadowy figures moved around. Excited, I hopped onto the portico and rang the bell, with Dad and Bess right behind me.

The door opened, and a genial-looking man in his fifties with a slim build, dark hair graying around the temples, and bright blue eyes smiled at me from the foyer. I stepped back, surprised by his resemblance to Dad. "May I help you?" he asked in an upper crust British accent, the kind that you hear royalty use on TV.

"Yes, I'm Nancy Drew, and this is my father, Carson Drew, and my friend Bess Marvin. Dr. Burnham sent us here to check on his house."

"Who?" the man said, sounding confused. "I'm afraid I don't know a Dr. Burnham. Anyway, as you can see, my house doesn't need checking," he added with a chuckle.

"Do you know Mrs. Elliott?" I asked him. "She's Dr. Burnham's housekeeper. Dr. Burnham's address is Fifty-three Banbury Square, and Mrs. Elliott lives at his house."

"Never heard of Mrs. Elliott," the man said. "As for the address, there are several nearby streets with the name Banbury. This is Banbury Square, but maybe you mean Banbury Row or Crescent."

Could I have misheard Dr. Burnham? But he wouldn't have written down "Square" if he'd meant "Row" or "Crescent." No way do those words sound alike.

A scuffing noise attracted my attention to the back of the foyer, where a plump, apple-cheeked woman scurried across with two silver candlesticks and a sil-

20

ver teapot. Mrs. Elliott? She was gone in a flash. The man fixed me with his gaze, as if nothing the least bit strange was happening in back of him, but why would the woman be carrying candlesticks and a teapot and hurrying as if she didn't want to be seen? Beyond the man's left shoulder was a cheerfully furnished living room with a telephone on a side table, bookshelves, and a fire. Seeing it, I got an idea.

"Um, could we use your phone? Or maybe your phone book?" I asked. "I mean, to double-check the address."

The man started and stepped back, his smile crumpling into a frown. "Allow perfect strangers into my 'ouse?" he grumbled, his accent slipping into cockney. "No way, miss." He slammed the door in our faces before I could open my mouth.

3

Crime Scene

That man is an imposter!" Bess exclaimed.

"My thoughts exactly," I said, exchanging shocked looks with Dad and Bess. "Anyway, let's not waste time checking the other streets named Banbury. Why don't we call Dr. Burnham? He needs to know that someone who doesn't even know his name is living in his house."

"I bet that locksmith didn't make a bad key," Dad said. "Those people must have had the locks changed."

A large red phone booth—a common sight in England—beckoned us from a nearby corner. Since our cell phones didn't work overseas, we were stuck with using pay phones. I dialed Dr. Burnham's number, hoping he'd be home at eight in the morning midwestern time. My hopes were rewarded when his quiet voice answered my call. After asking him how he was, I briefly described my encounter with the man at his house.

The instant I described the woman, Dr. Burnham cried, "That's Mrs. Elliott!"

"But who was the man?" I asked.

"I don't know," he replied anxiously. "Maybe Mr. Elliott. But I never met him, and she never described him."

"Do you think Mrs. Elliott changed the lock?" I asked.

"It sounds that way to me," Dr. Burnham said. "And why was she running around with my silver? Nancy, please call the police and get them over there immediately."

The moment we hung up, I did exactly as he asked.

"I'll have to speak directly with the homeowner, luv," a police woman told me. "Please tell him to contact us."

But when I called Dr. Burnham back, he didn't answer. I figured he must have just headed off to teach class. After leaving a message on his answering machine, I hung up, frustrated. The people in his house might clean it out by the time the police arrived there. What to do now?

Dad solved that dilemma. "Nancy, there's no way

we can help Dr. Burnham at this moment. We're just standing out in the rain and spinning our wheels. But I could use a nap, and I would suggest the same for you girls. So let's return to the hotel. Nothing like a good rest to freshen the mind after an all-night flight."

I sighed. Here we were in London with a mystery on our hands. Take a nap? No way! "I don't know, Dad. Sightseeing might freshen my mind too. Anything to take it off Dr. Burnham until I can reach him."

Dad sighed, sounding melancholy, resigned, and proud all at the same time. That sounds impossible, but Dad can juggle several contradictory thoughts. Did I mention he's a smart guy? "Nancy, I know you too well to expect you to rest while there's an unsolved mystery in the world," he said. "So go sightsee, and don't wait for me if you girls get hungry for dinner. But please promise me one thing. Don't go back to Fifty-three Banbury Square without the police. It's too dangerous."

But what was so risky about an older couple, if a bit grouchy, giving me the runaround? Still, he is my father, and I respected his concerns. One key part of our relationship is honesty.

"Okay, Dad," I said. "What if I promise not to let that couple know I'm at the house? Bess and I will be completely safe if we just sneak a look through the windows. Don't forget, Dr. Burnham is depending on us."

Dad threw me a fatherly look. "Nancy, I admire your determination, so I'm not going to stand in the way of what you think is right. Still, I want you to try to get the police to go with you."

"I will, Dad," I said, throwing my arms around him in a hug. "Now promise me you'll get some rest so we can all enjoy London together?"

Dad gave me the thumbs-up sign, then hailed a cab to take him, along with Bess's packages, back to the hotel. Bess and I decided to kill time visiting Westminster Abbey, the huge cathedral on the bank of the Thames River that's like British history in a nutshell. As we headed to the nearest subway train—called the Underground here and nicknamed the Tube—I saw strips of blue sky threading through the gray clouds overhead. The air was warm and humid, and Bess and I happily closed our umbrellas and shrugged off our raincoats.

Once at Westminster Abbey, we strolled through the enormous doors into one of the oldest and largest religious buildings in England. After grabbing some headphones for an audio tour, we learned that the Abbey had been founded in 1065 by St. Edward the Confessor, the last Saxon king. Then William the

Conqueror, the Norman who defeated the Saxons at the Battle of Hastings in 1066, was crowned king here later that year. According to our audio tour guide, the coronation tradition continues at Westminster Abbey to this day.

"Tombs of a zillion kings and queen are here," Bess commented, as we strolled through a side chapel guided by our audio tour. "Look over here at this one, Nancy. It's where both Queen Mary and Queen Elizabeth the First are buried. I can't believe they share a tomb. They were mortal enemies!"

"Yeah, Mary imprisoned Elizabeth, her own sister, and Elizabeth was worried Mary might have her killed," I said.

"Hmm, I wonder how they're getting along in there," Bess quipped, glancing at the tomb. "Maybe they've learned to forgive each other by now."

We wandered away from the royalty section and into the area commemorating poets and writers. Near the west door was a memorial to Sir Winston Churchill, England's leader during World War II. "It seems as if everyone you've ever heard of in England besides rock stars, fashion models, and chefs has a monument here," I said.

"Speaking of chefs, I'm kind of hungry, Nancy. How about a snack?"

"Okay. Then I'll try calling Dr. Burnham again.

But if he doesn't answer, let's check his house again, even if the police can't meet us there."

"But you promised your dad that you wouldn't go back without them."

"I promised Dad that we wouldn't let the Elliotts, or whoever they are, know we're at the house. But I told him we might look through the windows."

With help from the map in my guidebook, Bess and I found our way through quiet, rain-drenched streets to Dr. Burnham's neighborhood. Once there, we found a pub, the King's Castle. One thing I'd been noticing about London was that lots of the pubs and hotels had descriptive names, often sounding medieval and reminding me how old a country Britain was. Some of these places, from Westminster Abbey to humble neighborhood pubs, had been around for centuries. So far, I hadn't seen one mall, and that was just fine with me.

At the King's Castle Bess and I ordered sodas and a cheese plate, and before long we were snacking away happily. A group of men and women clustered around the bar, and several others sat at nearby tables. "Since we're so close to Dr. Burnham's house, I'm going to keep an ear out for local gossip," I told Bess between bites. "Maybe someone will let something slip about Mrs. Elliott or the house."

But my hopes were quickly dashed when a man

27

walked in leading a large gray and white sheepdog, its eyes hidden by a tangle of white curly hair. "Hello, cutie!" a woman commented, reaching out to pat the dog.

"His name is Gus," the owner remarked.

"What do you feed him to get such a fine soft coat?" an older man asked.

As the conversation stuck stubbornly to Gus and his ways, I said, "Somehow, Bess, I have a feeling we're not going to pick up any useful stuff about Dr. Burnham here."

Bess smiled, glancing at the adorable dog now asleep on the carpet by his owner. "Gus is a hot topic! Next to him, imposters and burglars don't stand a chance."

I checked my watch. "Wow! Time flies. I'll be right back, Bess. I'm going to find a phone and call Dr. Burnham."

"In the meantime, I'll get the bill," Bess offered.

A few minutes later I was back in my seat. "Dr. Burnham didn't answer his phone," I told Bess. "It's still late morning in River Heights, so I guess he's out teaching. Anyway, there's no chance the police will join us at his house now."

"That's okay," Bess said. "There are plenty of windows we can look through."

Bess and I paid our bill, then hurried to Dr. Burnham's house at the end of the street. Once there, we hid in some lilac bushes outside the living-room windows, which were dimly lit by the hall chandelier.

But the windows were just a little too high for us. As I strained to peek inside, Bess said, "Here, Nancy, let me give you a leg up." Cupping her hands, she hoisted me up while I grabbed the ledge to steady myself.

I almost fell over at the sight that greeted me. Not a stick of furniture was left in the once cheerful living room. Even the embers in the fire looked cold. The bookshelves lining the fireplace were empty. The house looked deserted. Gripping the window ledge so hard my knuckles went white, I threw Bess a look of total shock. What was going on at Dr. Burnham's?

4

Kidnapped!

Bess," I cried, leaping down. "We're too late! The furniture is gone." I pointed to the far side of the front door. "Here, let's look in those windows."

"Has the whole house been cleaned out?" Bess wondered.

We scurried through the bushes to the other set of windows. As Bess gave me another leg up, I steeled myself for an empty room. Fortunately, the dining room set looked undisturbed, but if Dr. Burnham had kept any silver there, it was long gone. My mind flashed back to the candlestick I'd seen the woman carrying earlier. Where was it now?

I jumped down. "The dining-room furniture is all there, Bess. At least I think so. No sign of any silver, though. But that empty living room is freaky."

"Poor Dr. Burnham," Bess said. "Who do you think those people were who answered the door?"

I shrugged. "Probably Mrs. Elliott and her husband, trying to rip off Dr. Burnham while he's away. Anyway, we've got to go to the police. They have to pay attention to us now."

We grabbed a cab, and five minutes later we'd arrived at the local police station. The officer in charge was Constable Reynolds, a bespectacled, heavyset man with a gruff but kindly manner. After explaining our story to him, I dialed Dr. Burnham's number from the phone on his desk. "Leave a message on his machine if he's not there," Constable Reynolds suggested, running a hand through his short white hair. "He can call me back on my direct line."

But when Dr. Burnham's live voice came through the receiver, I hesitated, dreading his reaction to my awful news. "Nancy!" he exclaimed. "Have you managed to contact the police yet?"

I explained the long, sad story. After a terrible pause, his strangled voice sputtered out, "My furniture, everything that I grew up with, photos, stuff from my grandparents . . . my books! Nancy, don't tell me all of that is gone!"

"I'm really sorry, Dr. Burnham." Those words seemed so lame, but what else could I say?

"But my books! How could they be gone? Did I mention that I own a rare edition of Shakespeare's *King Lear*? I don't even care that it's worth a lot of money. It's priceless to me."

"Dr. Burnham, please calm down," I said, trying my best to soothe him. "We'll do everything we can to find your stuff." His quiet, unruffled manner at the Moonbeam Diner reflected a totally different man from the anguished person I was speaking to now.

"Oh, Nancy, this is a bad dream," he continued. "If I'd had any idea those mysterious things happening in my house would lead to this, I would have gone to the police much sooner."

"I wish the police hadn't needed to speak with you before agreeing to check your house," I told him. "Anyway, I promise to find the people who did this to you. I guess that would be Mrs. Elliott."

"Your description fits her exactly, Nancy. I can't thank you enough for all you've done. If you wouldn't mind staying on the case, I'd be very grateful. Maybe you can track her down yet. In the meantime, I'll catch the next plane to England, as soon as I find a teaching substitute for my classes."

After we finished our conversation, Constable Reynolds got on the phone, asking Dr. Burnham some basic questions about his missing possessions, and details about Mrs. Elliott. Then Constable

Reynolds requested permission for a locksmith to open the house. Soon, they hung up, and the constable turned to Bess and me. "Well, girls, I understand Dr. Burnham wants you to help us solve this case. He told me you're an experienced detective, Nancy. So let's keep in touch and help each other as much as possible. The first thing I'm going to do is question Mrs. Elliott."

"But how will you know where to find her?" Bess asked. "Wasn't her last address Dr. Burnham's house?"

"What many people don't realize is that live-in housekeepers and nannies usually have permanent lodgings of their own," Constable Reynolds explained. "We'll start by locating hers. But even before we launch a search for this mysterious house-keeper, we need to examine the scene of the crime. Dr. Burnham's house."

"Do you mind if we come with you?" I asked. "Remember Dr. Burnham wants us to help you!"

The constable grinned. "Do please join us, Nancy. I was counting on you girls to find clues that we older folks might miss." After wiping his glasses with a handkerchief, he ordered a squad car to head to 53 Banbury Square for evidence gathering.

Once we'd arrived at Dr. Burnham's house, Bess and I waited with Constable Reynolds and two other officers while a locksmith opened the door.

Inside, the house held no obvious surprises. The living room was empty, just as it had been an hour ago, the hall chandelier was still on, and the dining room still had its furniture. But I found the silver candlesticks and teapot tossed on the kitchen counter, as if the thieves had left them there in a scramble to get out the door.

"Well, at least the professor didn't lose these," a young woman constable remarked. "The living room is the only one that seems to have been burglarized. Perhaps it had most of the valuables, or perhaps the thieves ran out of time."

We spent the next half hour looking for evidence. Or clues, as I like to say. Nothing stood out until I strolled through the dining room one last time before calling it quits for the night. A white triangular object poking out from underneath the sideboard caught my eye. Bending, I pulled out a sheaf of papers—a manuscript titled *The Scottish Play* by Augusta Dorrance. Could it have been left by the thieves? I glanced over my shoulder. Not a constable in sight. I pushed the manuscript under the bed with a good kick.

"Nancy!" Bess said, entering the room. I jumped guiltily before realizing she was alone. "Do you know what time it is? Eight o'clock already. Your dad may be awake and worrying about us."

"You're right, Bess. It's dinnertime, and I'm not even hungry. My inner clock is telling me it's more like midafternoon. Anyway, let's go back to the hotel and join Dad. We can start the investigation again tomorrow once we've rested."

We said good-bye to Constable Reynolds and promised to keep in touch, then hailed a cab to take us back to the White Swan Hotel. "I hope Dad hasn't been too worried about us," I said as I knocked on the door linking our two rooms. After getting no response, I added, "I wonder if he's still asleep."

But more knocking failed to rouse him. "Maybe he went out," I said. I felt a prickle of worry that I tried my best to squash. "I'm going to pick the lock." I dug in my purse for my trusty barrette. It wasn't the first time I'd used it to spring a door.

Three seconds later the door opened, and I stared in shock at Dad's room. Someone had trashed it! Furniture was overturned, Dad's clothes were strewn on the floor, and freakiest of all, Dad himself was missing!

5

A Mysterious Blonde

I **rushed into the** room with Bess right behind me. "Dad!" I called. No answer. I peeked into the open door of his bathroom. No one there. I cast a look over the demolished room, my head spinning. No way could Dad have just gone out for a walk or for dinner. The chaos here showed that he'd been forced from his room. What other explanation was there for the furniture and other things being thrown all over the place?

Bess and I traded horrified looks. I could hardly believe this was happening. And it wasn't a bad dream. I could pinch myself, but nothing would change the grim reality.

I took a deep breath. Staying calm in the face of danger while solving a case was easy compared to how I felt now. I mean, this was my own father missing! How could I even think straight while Dad might be hurt? But my best hope of finding him was by keeping calm and using my wits, like I did when I solved other mysteries. It's just that those didn't involve my own dad!

Bess put her arm around me and led me to the chair that hadn't been overturned. "Nancy, it's going to be okay. We'll find him. He can't be far. Just relax. Your dad needs every ounce of your brain power."

I sat down, forcing myself to get a grip, meeting Bess's concerned gaze gratefully. I took another breath, then scanned the room for information the way a detective would, not a frantic daughter. I noticed that his clothes formed a trail that led back to his overturned suitcase by the base of the luggage rack, as if he'd been surprised in the midst of unpacking.

"He obviously wasn't expecting his visitor," I said.

"Visitors, probably," Bess said, emphasizing the plural. "I doubt your father could have been overpowered by just one person."

"Unless the person had gigantic muscles or a weapon," I pointed out. "Though if the person had a weapon, I don't think there would have been a struggle like this."

The detective in me sloughed off the fear and frozen feeling I had a minute ago and started to go into overdrive. I inspected the lock on the front door, as well as the one on the door between our two rooms. "No marks on either of these doors," I commented, "no signs of a forced entry. Of course, there's nothing here that shows we picked the lock either."

"It was either a clever lock picker like you, Nancy, or your father willingly let the person in," Bess observed.

I nodded. "So even though Dad was forced out of the room, he may have opened the door himself."

"Which means he may have considered the person safe at first, and then got surprised when his visitor meant him harm," Bess said.

"Exactly," I confirmed. "Of course, the person could have had a hotel key and was waiting inside for Dad to come back." My eye caught the phone on the bedside table. "Hang on a second." I pushed redial and was immediately connected to room service.

"Room 405, where were you when I knocked?" a man's voice asked, sounding a bit peeved. "We prepared your fish and chips, and then no one answered your door."

I quickly explained the situation to the horrified room-service captain. "What time did Dad order dinner?" I asked.

"Six twenty-three precisely," the captain answered. "And the waiter delivered the meal at six forty-five.

But really, Miss Drew, your father couldn't be missing. He's probably out for a walk and got lost. He'll find his way back shortly, I'm certain."

I didn't feel like arguing, especially because I'd gotten the info I needed. Some people have a hard time accepting bad news, so they ignore the facts. I'm no fan of bad news either, but the only way to turn it into good news is to deal with it. I hung up the phone and turned to Bess.

"I bet Dad's attacker posed as room service, which means Dad went missing sometime between six twenty-three and six forty-five. Either someone in room service tipped the person off, or Dad's attacker was able to sneak into the kitchen and get the information. Whatever. Either way, Dad has been missing for about two hours." The impact of my words sank in and froze me with worry once again. Two hours! Dad may not even be in London anymore.

I couldn't let worry rule me. It's a sneaky thing, worry; it grabs you when you least expect it. I fought it by focusing on thoughts of Dad, Bess, and me happily reunited. *Soon,* I promised myself. "Let's hunt for more clues," I suggested.

Bess and I prowled around the room, scouting for anything out of the ordinary. It didn't take me long to find a wadded-up piece of paper near the mess of clothes by Dad's suitcase. Opening it up, I saw the name and address of a place called Books of Olde written in black fountain pen. Definitely not Dad's writing.

My mind flashed back to my lunch with Ned and Dr. Burnham. Wasn't Dr. Burnham's threatening note also written in black fountain pen? It's pretty uncommon to use fountain pens in the U.S.—ballpoints or felt tips are much more popular. The same was probably true in the U.K. So the person who kidnapped Dad may also have written Dr. Burnham's note.

"Hmm . . . Books of Olde," Bess said, peering over my shoulder. "I bet it's an old-book store."

"Probably," I agreed. "Anyway, this clue makes me think that whoever took Dad also wrote Dr. Burnham that note and stole his stuff." After explaining my observation about the similar inks, I added, "Also, Dr. Burnham lost his rare copy of *King Lear*. Maybe the person who stole it is trying to sell it to this store. But why would that person take Dad?" I sighed, pocketed the paper, and swept the room with one more gaze. "I think we're finished here, Bess. Let's go to the police and the American Embassy. I want everyone on the case."

And that included the hotel manager, who was dumbfounded when he heard our story. He assured us that none of the staff had seen anything unusual. No strangers lurking about at all. But he promised to stay alert for clues to Dad's disappearance and potential danger to me and Bess.

Two hours later Bess and I were back at the hotel, halfheartedly munching on room-service burgers. We'd only just realized that in all the chaos over Dad, we'd forgotten to eat dinner. But my mouth felt dry, and I pushed my meal away after barely a nibble. The unhappy fact was this: Dad was gone, and neither the American Embassy nor the police had any idea how to find him.

It was nice that both the embassy and the police had been friendly and willing to help. They'd been upset by our story and promised to get on the case pronto. The police vowed to warn all rare-book merchants to be on alert for the missing *King Lear* and to get the name and address of the person trying to sell it. They also promised to search the Internet for it. But the fact remained that Dad was gone. He might be cold and hungry. He might be hurt.

A wave of exhaustion hit me like a brick. I'd barely slept since the night before last in River Heights. I had to make sure my mind was clear for tomorrow. Somehow, Dad's disappearance and Dr. Burnham's mystery were related, I was sure. I just had to figure out how.

Just as we were moving our room-service tray out

into the hall, the phone rang. I flopped across my bed to answer it and recognized the voice of the hotel manager. "Ms. Drew," he announced, "an extra key to your father's room has been discovered missing. Possibly it was swiped from the cubbyhole behind the front desk while the clerk was briefly busy elsewhere. I've already notified the police."

I thanked the manager, then Bess and I put on our pj's and fell into an anxious sleep.

Sunlight flooded through the window, glancing off the dresser mirror, right into my eyes. I woke with a start, imagining that someone was shining a flashlight at me. And then I remembered Dad.

"It's okay, Nancy," Bess said soothingly, as if she read my thoughts. "We'll find him. I just know it. At least the rain has stopped. It actually looks really hot outside."

I jumped out of bed and pulled on some jeans, a blouse, and boots. "You'll roast in those," Bess warned as she dug a black tank top, green miniskirt, and pink striped flip-flops from her suitcase. "Check out the weather."

"Wow, Bess, you're right," I said as I opened one of the French windows onto a small balcony. "It's like eighty-five degrees. What a change from yesterday!"

"Definitely not your typical English weather,"

Bess remarked. "Well, the English might not be used to it, but it's awesome for us. Following leads to your Dad will be much easier without worrying about getting soaked."

"Right, Bess!" I said as I changed into cotton slacks and sneakers. No matter how fearful I was about Dad, I was determined to adopt a positive attitude. I'd solved so many mysteries in the past, and I would solve this one. No other choice. No other option.

"Anyway," I added, "let's head back to the police and see whether they've found anything. We can pick up something to eat on our way."

Soon we were sitting in the police station, digesting Constable Reynolds's harsh words that no progress had been made in his attempt to find Dad. Early that morning before Bess and I were up, an officer had dusted Dad's room for fingerprints and interviewed the hotel staff. None of the fingerprints matched police databases, and they didn't match hospital databases either. My tiny hope that Dad might be in the hospital with temporary amnesia was dashed.

"What's more," Constable Reynolds said as he continued his summary of the police work so far, "Mrs. Elliott hasn't been seen by her landlady or neighbors for at least a week, though that's to be expected since she lives at Dr. Burnham's. We poked around her residence this morning."

"Any thoughts on who the man at Dr. Burnham's might be?" I asked.

"We believe that was Mr. Elliott. Your description of him, Nancy, matches his neighbors' descriptions. It turns out he's not estranged from his wife after all. He hasn't been seen either, not for the past two days. Since he supposedly doesn't live at Dr. Burnham's, that news is somewhat alarming. Makes me think the two skipped out together somewhere, possibly with your father."

"Do you know what Mr. Elliott does for a living?" Bess asked.

"He's retired, but he used to be a security guard at the British Museum," Constable Reynolds said. "Anyway, girls, I'm sorry I don't have better news for you, but I promise to keep in close touch with you. We've also posted a police scout near the Elliotts' flat, who will nab them if they show up." He scrawled an address on a piece of paper and handed it to me. "Here's the Elliotts' address in case you want to double-check their flat for clues. We police do our best, but no one is perfect."

As he spoke, I struggled to keep my emotions in check so I could focus on the case, but it was a hard fight. I mean, what was Dad doing now? Was he okay or was he hurt? Trapped, maybe? The possibilities paralyzed me. I bit my lip. I had to stifle my thoughts and forge ahead. Next stop: Books of Olde.

After thanking Constable Reynolds and assuring him we'd be in touch throughout the day, Bess and I hopped into a taxi and gave the driver the address of Books of Olde. "That's on the other side of the river Thames," the driver commented. "Not far from the Globe Theatre."

As the driver threaded his way through traffic toward one of the bridges spanning the river Thames, we passed Buckingham Palace, the queen's official residence, where guards in tall black hats and red uniforms stood sentry at the gates. Their stiff poses and heavy uniforms looked uncomfortable on this hot day.

"I know they're real," Bess declared, "though they look more like life-size toy soldiers than actual people."

"I don't think they're even allowed to move," I said. "Royal protocol, I guess." Buckingham Palace was majestic and massive as the cab raced by. As soon as we found Dad, I'd be able to enjoy London sights again.

Soon we crossed a bridge over the Thames, which

overlooked the Houses of Parliament and Big Ben, the huge clock tower on the London skyline. Once on the other side, we zipped down narrow stone streets that felt as if they had been built in the Middle Ages. But the cab driver seemed undaunted as he hurtled around a tight corner and stopped next to a Tudor-style building. A wooden sign with colorful letters spelling "Books of Olde" hung above a tiny door that looked as if it had been built for a hobbit, not a human. At five foot seven, I had to duck a bit as we entered.

Once inside, Bess and I came face-to-face with a small gnarled man with wild shoulder-length white hair. His long mustache, resembling walrus tusks, drooped down each side of his face. "Welcome to Books of Olde. May I help you girls?" he asked hoarsely, his mustache puffing upward as he spoke.

I glanced around the shop, which was filled with overflowing shelves crammed with musty ancient books. A pleasant smell of leather, paper, and lemon-flavored tea wafted through the room, stirred up by a creaky ceiling fan that sounded as if it had last been used during World War I. "Hot day, what?" the man added.

"It sure is," I agreed.

He chuckled. "I don't think we've had May weather this warm for, I don't know . . . Actually, I think I've got an almanac that'll give us a weather history."

I didn't want to be impolite by cutting him short, but I'd come to find Dad, not weather records! Worry made me blunt. "Sir, we're planning to browse in your store, but first I have a question. Do you know anyone named Dr. Burnham or Mr. and Mrs. Elliott? Dr. Burnham is a professor at the University of London."

The man pursed his lips thoughtfully. "I've never heard of any of those people. Authors, are they?"

"Dr. Burnham is," I replied. And then I remembered Dr. Burnham's stolen books. "Do you happen to have a rare edition of *King Lear*?"

"No, I don't. Sorry, miss. But I have many other worthy Shakespeare plays if you'd care to browse," he said with a grand sweep of his hand. "A rare edition of *Macbeth* is yours for the asking."

I smiled. "I'm interested only in *King Lear*." Taking my notebook from my purse, I jotted my name and number at the White Swan Hotel on a piece of paper and handed it to him. "Would you mind contacting me if anyone tries to sell you one?"

Before he could answer, the shop door opened,

and a beautiful young woman with long honey gold hair waltzed inside. She looked like a grown-up version of Alice in Wonderland.

"Why, if it isn't Augusta Dorrance!" the old man cried. "Cheerio!"

I perked up at the name. It sounded so familiar. Wait! Wasn't Augusta Dorrance the author of the manuscript I'd found on Dr. Burnham's floor?

6

Ghost Stories

Bess's gaze caught mine. I whispered, "Let's pretend to browse. This conversation might get interesting."

We strolled over to some bookshelves in a nearby corner where I stared blindly at several tattered leather spines. The titles of the books were one big blur as I focused my attention on Augusta and the store owner, hoping for good eavesdropping acoustics. I immediately got my wish.

"Cheerio to you, sir!" Augusta replied enthusiastically. "How have you been?" She had a throaty voice and a slinky way of standing that reminded me of an old–time movie star as Augusta leaned on a pile of books on the old man's desk. She wore a blue miniskirt, and "mini" was definitely the operative word.

The man fanned himself with his knobby hand. "I could use a bit of air-conditioning in the shop, but otherwise I can't complain. What can I do for you today, my dear Augusta?"

"Do you have any used copies of *Macbeth*? My dog ate mine," she added with a giggle.

"Now you're pulling my leg," he said, chuckling. "Your dog is old and practically toothless. You've brought him into my shop on many occasions, and he wouldn't harm a book to save his life. Is that what you used to tell your teachers when you didn't hand in homework—that your dog ate it?" he added playfully.

"You know what a hard worker I am," she declared with a pout. Even though she was acting kind of silly, I could tell Augusta was serious about her work. A sharp glint of determination shared space with the teasing expression in her eyes. "In fact, I just recently finished a play," she added. "It's based on *Macbeth*."

"Shakespeare continues to inspire you, my dear?"

"Of course. Shakespeare is the greatest playwright who ever lived, in my opinion, that is."

"Well, many people agree," the man said. "So tell me about your new play. How is it based on *Macbeth*? Are there witches in it?"

Augusta smiled. "The witches in my play aren't

like old crones," she replied. "They're attractive young women who are chefs in a fancy London restaurant. And the only prediction they make is that they won't all marry the same man, a chap they all love."

"Sounds funny—unlike *Macbeth*," the man observed.

"I tried to make it entertaining. I hope I succeeded," Augusta said modestly. "If I ever get it produced, I'll let you know. It's called *The Scottish Play*."

I knew that actors had a long tradition of never mentioning the title of *Macbeth* for fear that it would bring them bad luck. Instead they nicknamed it *The Scottish Play*.

"I like the title!" the man said, twinkling. "Now let's get back to business. You said you need a used copy of *Macbeth*? I've got a rare edition, if that interests you."

Augusta frowned. "I'm on a budget. A rare edition would be way too expensive for me. A used paperback is all I need."

"Sorry, love, I'm all out of them," the man said, shaking his head. "Check back in a few days. I'm always getting used books in. Rare editions, of course, are harder to come by. They sell briskly, though, when I do get them in."

Augusta flashed him a high-wattage smile. I had

no idea what her game was, but her style was more film star than impoverished playwright. "Well, good-bye for now," she crooned. "Nice chatting." And with a swish of her miniskirt, she strolled out the door.

Unfortunately, she never mentioned losing her manuscript. Or Dr. Burnham's name. Was she even aware that her manuscript—or a copy of it—had been in his house? I knew I could catch up and ask her those questions. But following her at a distance might be a better idea. Maybe she'd lead us to Dad, or to his kidnappers. Anyway, I could always ask her questions later.

I whispered my plan to Bess, and we headed for the door.

"Not so fast, girls," the old man said, lowering his arm in front of us. "We haven't finished our conversation about the rare edition of *King Lear* that you wanted."

I smiled weakly. Information about rare *King Lear* editions sounded tempting—it might clue us in to Dad—but so did following Augusta.

"I will certainly get in touch with you if one comes my way," he assured me. "However, I must warn you not to get your hopes up. Those editions aren't called rare for nothing."

"Thanks so much," I said, edging toward the door. Bess and I had to get out or we'd lose Augusta for sure. "I'll be at that phone number I gave you for the next few days."

Once outside, Bess and I scanned the street for Augusta. "I hope we haven't lost her," I said.

"There!" Bess said, pointing to the right. Augusta's long shiny hair caught the sunlight just as she rounded a far corner. "Maybe we can catch her if we run fast."

We raced down the street, Bess's flip-flops slapping hard against the ancient cobblestones. There was no doubt that on medieval sidewalks sneakers ruled.

Soon Bess and I were barreling around the corner, scouting the wide plaza in front of us for signs of Augusta. Beyond it, the river Thames gleamed in the bright sunlight. A sightseeing boat, bustling with passengers, bobbed in front of us by the dock. A flash of gold against the silvery river caught my attention— Augusta, skipping down the last ten feet of sidewalk and sashaying onto the crowded boat!

"Let's get tickets, Bess. I want us to be on that boat when it leaves." We headed to a nearby ticket kiosk and bought two tickets. Seconds later we hopped on board.

"Phew, just in time," Bess said breathlessly as the boat captain pulled up the ramp and blew the whistle. "By the way, Nancy, did you catch where we're going?"

"Nope," I said. "But at least we're with Augusta. Anyway, good running, Bess. You could win a marathon in flip-flops."

Bess grinned. "I'd do anything to help you find your dad, Nancy."

A voice boomed over the loudspeaker. "Ladies and gents, welcome on board the *Victorian Princess* bound for the Tower of London. This is Captain Barclay, your sightseeing host for the day." He continued on, pointing out various points of interest on either side of us. With Big Ben and the Houses of Parliament across the water and the dome of St. Paul's Cathedral down river, London had a majestic atmosphere to it that fit its royal history.

But I didn't have time to think about the view or the city's history. I was too busy worrying about Dad. Also, I had to watch Augusta, who was deep in conversation with a tall handsome young guy with shoulder-length dreadlocks and a jovial gleam in his deep brown eyes. Sitting next to Augusta near the prow of the boat, he leaned toward her whenever she spoke, as if hanging on her every word. What could they be talking about? Even though Bess and I were sitting six feet away, there was no way I could hear them with the loudspeaker blaring and the wind blowing. I was tempted to get closer, but I didn't dare.

The boat chugged along. Soon, it swept to the opposite side of the Thames and approached a huge forbidding stone fortress that made my stomach sink—the infamous Tower of London. Resembling a giant prison with crenellated towers similar to the rooks in chess, it looked as solid as an iceberg, except gray. With tiny slits for windows, how could anyone have stood being cooped up there? I shivered, thinking of all the English political prisoners who had been locked up there before meeting their doom at the hand of the executioner. Well, all that was in the past, at least. And then I thought of Dad, locked up somewhere else—but in the present! I bit my lip. No matter how hard things got, I had to keep up my hopes.

"I wonder why Augusta wants to go to the Tower?" Bess said, cutting into my thoughts. "I mean, she's not a tourist or anything—she lives here."

I agreed that Augusta was acting strangely. Why was she looking at the London sights as if she'd never set eyes on them before? "She's behaving as if this were her first time on the Thames," I said.

"Well, maybe it is," Bess said. "Haven't you heard of all those New York City residents who have never visited the Statue of Liberty? Maybe she's like that."

"And what about that guy, Bess? Do you think he's her boyfriend?"

Before Bess could answer, the boat scraped against the dock and came to a shuddering stop near some ancient stone stairs. Moments later Bess and I were in the Tower compound behind Augusta and her friend, having given our tickets to one of the guards.

"I feel sorry for those guards all dressed up in their wool uniforms on this hot day," Bess remarked as we strolled inside. We picked up a couple of brochures that told us that the guards, nicknamed Beefeaters, wore their heavy wool uniforms as part of the Tower tradition. Their flushed faces, covered with sweat, looked pained but determined as they cheerfully gave directions to tourists who filed past them into the ancient battlement. "I'm surprised they don't get heatstroke," Bess added.

"Fortunately for them, the weather's not usually this hot," I commented.

Bess glanced at her brochure. "The history of the Tower sounds incredibly gory. There's a section called the Bloody Tower where the two little princes were murdered by Richard III so they wouldn't threaten his throne. I've always thought that story was so sad." Turning a page, she added, "Apparently, many of the rooms in the Tower are haunted."

"No wonder," I said, studying my brochure. "Sir Walter Raleigh, the famous Elizabethan explorer, died here too, and so did two of Henry the Eighth's six wives, Anne Boleyn and Catherine Howard."

"Six wives! Two executed?" Bess exclaimed. "Why would anyone marry someone with that track record?"

I shrugged. "I guess each wife thought she'd be an exception."

Bess frowned, her blue eyes peering through the crowd. "I hate to say this, Nancy, but I don't see Augusta anymore."

"I do. She and her friend are heading into the Jewel House." I pointed to a swish of long blond hair and dreadlocks disappearing through an entrance on our left. Even while examining my brochure, I'd kept an eye on Augusta, who'd been threading her way through the crowd, arm in arm with her friend. I wasn't about to take my eyes off her when there was even a small chance she could lead me to information about Dad.

We headed into the Jewel House behind Augusta and crowds of other tourists. Once inside, we paused for a moment to absorb the room's splendor. The gallery had a radiance about it from the display of emeralds, rubies, diamonds, and sapphires set into crowns, necklaces, robes, swords, and scepters. "This whole room glitters," Bess said, marveling at a sapphire-and-diamond crown that reminded me of stars on a cold winter night. The gallery had a hushed atmosphere, as if visitors couldn't find words to describe the spectacular jewels that had adorned kings and queens throughout English history.

"Look at this ruby choker," Bess said, strolling toward a small necklace with rubies the color of cranberry juice, "and that tiara," she added, pointing out a golden tiara with emeralds gleaming from it as green as a tiger's eyes.

I went through the motions of looking, but I couldn't really take in the sights. It was obvious I'd have to come back here once I found Dad. Then I could really enjoy it.

All this time I'd kept half an eye on Augusta, when suddenly a tour group filled the space between us. "Bess," I said, grabbing her arm, "we've got to keep up with Augusta!" But by the time we edged past the group, Augusta and her friend were nowhere to be seen.

Bess and I hurried outside and scanned the grassy square, but there was still no sign of them. "She must have gone into a different tower," I guessed. I studied the map inside my brochure, then pointed to a nearby door. "I think that's where Mary, Queen of Scots, was imprisoned by her cousin, Queen Elizabeth. Maybe she went in there."

"Let's check it out," Bess said.

Once inside, we hurried up a narrow spiral staircase winding to the prison cells. A cold feeling of impending doom clung to me as the clammy walls seemed to press upon us, as if we were suffocating in the coils of some giant snake. I could almost hear the despairing voices of ancient prisoners who had spent their final moments in this place. A fleeting thought went through my mind before I made myself squash it: What was Dad doing now? Wherever he was, I hoped he hadn't been imprisoned in a place like this.

The cell upstairs was empty. And then a high-pitched quaking voice filtered through the silence. "This is Mary, Queen of Scots, talking to you from the grave. Nancy Drew, Bess Marvin, your lives will soon end like mine!"

7

Danger at the Top

"**W**hat's that?" Bess said, jumping.

I whipped around the stairway corner. No one was there, but someone could easily have sneaked behind the curved walls and slipped downstairs unseen. "I bet it was Augusta sending us some cheesy fake ghost message. Actually, Bess, that warning is good news. It means we must be on the right track—the track that will lead us to Dad!"

"True," Bess said. "Augusta wouldn't feel she needs to threaten us if we weren't close to discovering an important clue."

We popped down the stairs and back outside. A familiar blond figure was inspecting a plaque describing the history of Tower Green, a grim place where many royals had met their untimely end.

Bess and I exchanged relieved looks. At least we'd found Augusta, although for some reason she was without her friend. We hurried closer, keeping a safe distance so she wouldn't notice us.

The early afternoon sunlight blasted down on us, making me feel like a wilted flower. I mean, was this England, or the Sahara Desert? Bess's face flushed a bright cherry red from the heat, though my friend would never complain. Bess is an awesome sport, especially when helping me solve a mystery. Especially when the mystery is my missing dad!

Augusta began to wander toward the fortress gate. "Let's go, Bess," I said. "I don't want to lose her again." Bess and I followed Augusta up a hill to a nearby Tube station. Soon we were descending a long escalator to the train platform deep below. I knew that during World War II, when London was being bombed by the Germans, Londoners would take refuge from the Blitz in Tube stations. This escalator seemed to go on and on, deep into the earth. I bit my lip as we descended. These Tube stations might have served as sanctuaries during the war, but I wouldn't feel safe again until I'd found Dad.

Once on the platform, we only had to wait a few seconds before the train clattered down the track with a whoosh of wind. Its doors slid open, and Augusta hopped on, with Bess and me behind her. I didn't dare take my eyes off her. She was my only lead to Dad.

Bess and I took seats close to Augusta, but not too close. "I wonder what happened to her friend?" Bess asked, shooting me a puzzled look.

"Maybe he had to go back to work."

After a few more stops, Augusta changed trains. Bess and I were her shadows. Finally Augusta exited the train at Westminster station, which I recognized from the day before when we visited the Abbey.

Up on the street, the sun beat onto us like a barbecue, even though it was beginning to slant toward the west. I bought a bottle of water from a sidewalk vendor, took a sip, then stuck it in my purse in case I got thirsty later.

Augusta headed toward the Thames between Parliament and Westminster Abbey. "What tourist attraction do you think she'll lead us to next?" Bess wondered. Instead of going toward either building, Augusta hurried over the bridge to the river's south bank, where a gigantic Ferris wheel called the London Eye rose above the water. Hordes of tourists regularly flock to the Eye for a bird's-eye view of the city.

"I guess that answers your question, Bess," I said. "Next stop for Augusta is the London Eye."

"But why is she doing all these touristy things?" Bess asked.

I shrugged, feeling my first pinprick of doubt about following Augusta. Maybe it was a waste of time. Yes, her manuscript had been found at Dr. Burnham's house, and yes, she'd visited Books of Olde, whose address had been dropped by Dad's kidnappers. She'd also been near enough to give us that fake warning at the Tower. But wouldn't we be better off hunting for the Elliotts? They were more directly tied to Dr. Burnham's burglary. I hesitated, then made up my mind. We'd come this far—we might as well discover whether Augusta was a red herring or a suspect worthy of the name.

"I assume the Eye is air-conditioned," Bess said, breaking into my thoughts.

I gazed up at the huge wheel. Instead of chairs like a regular Ferris wheel, the Eye had capsules similar to ski gondolas. If the capsules hadn't been air-conditioned, the passengers would definitely have roasted by now.

Augusta stopped at the end of the ticket line. After allowing some people to go between her and us so we wouldn't be too obvious, Bess and I stepped in line too. Fortunately, the line moved fast, and soon we were at the head of it. The next capsule was open and waiting for passengers as it swung slowly across the platform. A group of people filed into it, including Augusta.

Bess and I had to make it on! But just as our turn came, the man in charge of the doors stopped the line—at us.

"Wait!" I cried. "You've got to let us onto that car."

"It's a bit crowded," the operator said firmly. "People want space to move around in this heat."

"But our friends are on it," I protested. "Plus, there are only us two, and we don't take up much room. Please?"

The operator frowned. "Okay, miss, since you ask so nicely," he said. With a sweep of his arm, he motioned us onto the car.

The instant the door slid shut, cool air poured across my shoulders and neck, perking me up.

"This place feels great!" Bess said happily, taking a seat on a spacious wooden bench across from Augusta. "And it's not crowded at all." Bess was right. Besides us, there were twelve other tourists plus Augusta. We had plenty of space to move about or sit.

The movement of the capsule was barely perceptible as it inched its way above the city. I felt as if I was flying, like in *Peter Pan*, with the famous London skyline—Big Ben, Parliament, St. Paul's—spread out like a toy city far below. If only I had X-ray vision and could spot Dad. I felt a shiver of dread. What if he wasn't even in London anymore?

"Look, Nancy, in the capsule behind us!" Bess cried. "It's a wedding."

Everyone in our capsule pressed their noses against the glass to get a better view of the wedding—the bride in her white satin dress and the groom in his black tuxedo, exchanging vows above the city. A teenage bridesmaid wearing a pink tulle dress that accented her long dark hair looked on, while two flower girls, also in pink tulle, whispered excitedly to each other. Besides the minister, who presided over the scene in his black robe and white collar, there were only about three other couples, probably parents and friends. Colorful bouquets of pink and white carnations and white baby's breath covered the benches and made for a cheery scene.

The platinum ring sparkled in the sunlight as the groom placed it on the bride's finger. But just as she drew up her hand to admire it, the Eye seemed to stop. I looked toward Parliament and saw that I was right—we weren't moving anymore.

"Have we stopped?" Bess asked.

"I'm really hot," Augusta mumbled, fanning herself with her Tower brochure, which she'd taken from her purse. "I think the air-conditioning has stopped too."

"Maybe there's been a blackout," a gray-haired man guessed.

"That would be awful!" Augusta cried, terror clouding her sapphire blue eyes.

"Or maybe something is wrong with the machinery of the Eye," Bess said. Augusta's worried gaze flew to Bess, who added reassuringly, "Don't worry—if that's the case, I'm sure a mechanic is on hand to fix the problem quick. Maybe it's just a short circuit. Or maybe there's a gear that's broken. Anyway, even if the air-conditioning stopped, the cars are ventilated. We may get hot, but we won't suffocate."

I smiled at Bess. It's just like her to instantly wrestle with complicated mechanical problems. My friend may be a fashion hound, but she also knows her engines.

By now, despite the vents, the car was steaming hot. The air reminded me of a dishwasher during its heating cycle—almost too thick to breathe. Below us, the wedding party looked as wilted as their bouquets. The bride shot the groom a worried look as guests started to fan themselves with their wedding programs.

"I must say I'm feeling like a boiled egg!" Augusta exclaimed, her eyes meeting mine as she frantically fanned herself. Before I could respond, her eyes rolled back, making eerie white crescents in her face before they fluttered closed. Without speaking another word, she crumpled into a sweaty heap on the floor!

8

Don't Mess with Tea

I **took my water bottle** from my purse and splashed some on Augusta's face. Then I soaked a tissue with more water and gently pressed it on her forehead.

Augusta's eyes popped open. "What happened?" she asked, curiously looking at Bess, who was inspecting the capsule for a way to let in more air.

"You fainted," I replied. Propping her head up, I tilted the bottle of water toward her lips. She sipped the water delicately, like a cat lapping milk, then took a long deep gulp of the dense air.

A cool blast of air-conditioning suddenly blew through the capsule, and everyone lifted toward it like flowers to the sun. Ever so slightly, the Eye began to inch downward again as if nothing had happened. A woman in our capsule gave a sheepish giggle of relief, while in the wedding car, the teenage brides-maid shot a thumbs-up sign to the flower girls and the bride.

"There's an old saying that rain on your wedding day is good luck," Bess said, kneeling next to Augusta and me. "Maybe that includes getting stuck on the London Eye."

I smiled. "Maybe." Meanwhile I examined Augusta's face for signs that she was getting color back and feeling better. But as I peered more closely at her, she suddenly pushed me away.

"Please stop staring at me," Augusta said tartly.

"We were just trying to make sure you're okay," Bess declared. "You should see a first-aid person once we get down. The Eye should have someone on hand."

"I can take care of myself, thank you. I don't need help."

Bess frowned indignantly. "But if Nancy hadn't given you water, you might still be out cold on the floor." Bess is normally sweet and mild mannered, but she's not a girl to let an ungrateful comment slip by, especially when it might be hurtful to a friend.

A flicker of guilt crossed Augusta's face. "Sorry, girls," she said with a sigh. "I didn't mean to snap. It's just that I've been under a lot of stress lately. Please forgive me."

"Only if you'll let us take you out to lunch," I said. "I'd like to make sure you're okay before you go on alone."

"What a nice offer! It's really not necessary, though. I'll be fine. But I confess I'm a bit hungry, and it would be marvelous to eat something. But let me treat you. It's the least I can do. I can't believe I was so rude to you. Of course," she added in a teasing voice, "it's not my style to go places with strangers. But if it's a public place . . ."

"How about Fortnum and Mason?" Bess suggested. "I read about it in our guidebook and it sounds awesome."

Augusta brightened. "Fortnum and Mason is lovely. It's an enormous gourmet grocery store with a couple of restaurants in it. The downstairs tearoom serves ice-cream sundaes that will be perfect on a day like today."

"That's iced tea, I hope," Bess said.

Even with the Eye's air conditioner working, we were still pretty hot. In any case, I'd go to a place that served nothing but boiling hot soup if that meant I'd get to spend time with Augusta. How else would I learn how her manuscript ended up on Dr. Burnham's floor? I had to follow whatever leads might take me to Dad, no matter how slim they seemed.

"By the way," Bess said, extending her hand to Augusta. "I'm Bess Marvin, and this is my friend Nancy Drew."

"And I'm Augusta Dorrance. Pleased to meet you both."

Seconds later we returned to ground level and hopped off the Eye. The wedding party, chatting away happily, spilled out of the capsule directly behind us.

"Daniela," one of the flower girls said to the teenage bridesmaid, "why don't you ask someone? You're the brave one."

Ask who what? As Daniela strode over to a nearby security guard, I saw no reason not to follow her.

Daniela, a lively girl of about fourteen, introduced herself to the guard. "Hello, sir, I'm Daniela Ramirez. Maybe you can answer my question. I want to know why the Ferris wheel stopped, and the air-conditioning, too. Did the electricity break?"

"Miss, those are excellent questions," the guard said, smiling down at her. "You see, the warm day prompted an energy surge in the vicinity of the Eye, knocking out power to the area for a few minutes. I'm sorry if it caused you any discomfort."

"Well, my sister, the bride, wasn't too happy," Daniela said. "But she'll remember her wedding forever as kind of an adventure, don't you think?"

"I do think so, miss," the guard said kindly. "Give my congratulations to your sister and brother-in-law."

Daniela thanked him, then headed back to her group to tell them the news. Meanwhile Bess and Augusta had struck up a conversation with the bride and groom, and before too long we'd all introduced ourselves, myself and Daniela included.

"This hot weather has surprised everyone," the bride commented, adjusting her veil to allow more air flow. "I don't think anyone is quite ready for it this early in the season. Thank goodness we're honeymooning in Norway. On an island near the Arctic Circle."

"Elisa, shh," Daniela joked, "you're supposed to keep honeymoon plans secret. That's traditional." Turning to us, she added, "It was really nice meeting you all. Hope you have a good visit to London, Nancy and Bess. And Augusta, I hope you feel better."

We thanked her and wished the bride and groom many happy returns. Then Bess, Augusta, and I walked toward the bridge to hail a cab.

"If you're feeling faint, a taxi is better than the Tube," I said to Augusta once we were on our way to Fortnum & Mason.

"Oh, I'm feeling much better," Augusta replied.

"Still, I'm glad we took a cab. The Tube can get really crowded, enough to make the strongest person feel a bit woozy."

She did seem a whole lot better, and by the time we were sitting at a table in the downstairs tearoom at Fortnum & Mason, Augusta was positively bubbly. If she wasn't a suspect, I would definitely like her, but for now, I needed to reserve judgment and observe her. I also had to question her discreetly.

"Let's see," Augusta said, studying the menu. "It's already past three o'clock. I basically skipped lunch. Maybe instead of an ice-cream sundae I should get tea with all the works."

"Nancy and I haven't eaten yet, either," Bess said. "The works sounds good to me. Is that high tea?"

"High tea is actually a big meal eaten in the early evening," Augusta explained. "It's popular on farms where people have to keep working into the evening, so they need a hearty meal around six o'clock. But most tea drinkers take it around four o'clock with little sandwiches and cookies and such. Quite frankly, I'm so busy these days, I'm lucky if I get a drink of water in the afternoon, much less tea. Anyway, even though we're not having high tea today, please don't feel as if you have to skimp."

"Skimp? No way," Bess said firmly. "It's not every day we come to Fortnum and Mason."

"So where are you girls from?" Augusta asked. Bess and I took turns telling her about River Heights and how we'd recently arrived in London, leaving out the part about Dr. Burnham's house and Dad's disappearance.

As the waiter took our orders, I planned strategy. I studied Augusta, who seemed as cheerful as a kid as she ordered tea, cucumber sandwiches, scones, and strawberry jam. But how was I going to ask her about her manuscript without putting her on the defensive and ruining her mood? If she was guilty and learned that we knew she'd been at Dr. Burnham's, she might suddenly leave the table. In which case, I'd be just as far away from finding Dad as ever. Maybe if we buttered her up, she might inadvertently spill some important information.

"Augusta," I said, "was that you I saw at the Tower of London earlier today? I remember seeing an attractive blond woman who could have been your double touring it. But this person was acting as if she'd never visited the Tower before."

Happy surprise flashed across her face. "But that *was* me, Nancy," she cried. "What a coincidence!"

"So are you a visitor to London too?" I asked.

"Oh, no. I've lived here all my life. But I'm writing a play about London landmarks, so I've been researching them. Today was my day for the Tower

73

and the Eye. Next time, I'll visit some museums."

"You're a playwright?" Bess asked. "That's really cool. I've been taking a course on Shakespeare's comedies, and I can't wait to see a production at the Globe Theatre."

"Will the coincidences never stop?" Augusta said, throwing up her hands. "I'm director of a production of *Romeo and Juliet* at the Globe. It's been staged every few days for the past month, in repertory."

Now it was my turn to be impressed. Augusta was no fly-by-night playwright scribbling away in some attic, hoping that someday a crumb of recognition might be tossed her way. She was already a director at one of London's most famous theaters, rubbing shoulders with the most eminent English theater professionals. Could she really have something to do with Dad's disappearance? Maybe. Maybe not. Anyway, I've known some pretty unlikely criminals in my time.

"*Romeo and Juliet*?" Bess exclaimed. "I love that play!"

"Even though it's not a comedy?" Augusta asked.

Bess grinned. "Even Shakespeare's tragedies have comic parts in them. And *Romeo and Juliet* is so romantic."

"It's one of my favorites too." Brightening, Augusta added, "Listen, girls, tomorrow evening at six thirty is the final performance. Would you like to see it?" Fishing in her purse, she drew out a pair of tickets and handed them to us. "I keep a few of these on hand for each performance. Please take them and enjoy yourselves. I'll be interested to know how you like it."

"But please let us pay you for them," Bess urged.

"Don't be silly. These tickets are on me."

After we thanked Augusta, I asked, "So you're both a playwright and a director? No wonder you're so busy."

"That's me, darling," Augusta said theatrically. "I multitask. But yes, I'm in the theater business. Directing, playwriting—I love it all. Except I don't fancy being on stage."

Augusta's glamour-girl looks made her seem like a perfect actress type, not a typical writer, content to work by herself all day. Still, as I've mentioned, people can surprise me. Especially criminals.

"So what kind of plays do you write?" I asked.

"All my plays have been inspired by Shakespeare," Augusta replied. "My most recent play is a takeoff of *Macbeth* called *The Scottish Play*. Did you know that superstitious actors actually call *Macbeth* 'The Scottish Play'?"

"What happens if they say *Macbeth* by mistake?" Bess asked.

"All sorts of ghastly things," Augusta said, her blue eyes snapping. "Anyway, the research I did today was for my final draft."

"Speaking of coincidences, I found a manuscript called *The Scottish Play* yesterday," I said. "It was on the floor of a friend's house, a professor we know in America."

Augusta turned pale. "What's the professor's name?" she asked in a stricken tone.

"Dr. Samuel Burnham."

Augusta's face went from white to a sickly grayish pallor. Her eyes seemed to swim in her face. I leaned forward, ready to catch her in case she fainted again. "That was my first draft," she moaned. "How did he ever get hold of a copy?"

"So, you know Dr. Burnham?" Bess asked.

"He was my professor at the University of London," Augusta whispered. She focused on Bess and me as if seeing us for the first time. "But how do you girls know him?"

Before I had time to fudge an answer, our waiter arrived with our food. All conversation stopped as he set down iced tea and plates of scones, cookies, and miniature sandwiches for each of us. "Ladies, please let me know if I can get you anything else," he offered before moving off to another table.

The scone on my plate was still warm, and a delicious bakery smell wafted up from it. It made sense to eat the scone first, while it was still warm.

I picked it up. A folded piece of paper, speckled with melted grease, lay on the plate where the scone had been. I glanced at Augusta and Bess, but they were too busy with their own food to notice anything strange about mine.

I opened the paper, frowning down at an eight-line poem that I read in a flash, bad rhymes and all:

Nancy Drew, you need a clue.
If you want to find your father, here's what you do:
I'd like us to meet on Carnaby Street
At a shop called Todd.
It's really mod.
At the end of the day,
At the sun's last ray,
Be there, or beware.

9

Clued Out

What's that, Nancy?" Augusta asked innocently. "Did the kitchen staff leave something on your plate?"

I stared at her. She couldn't have planted this note, could she? She'd been sitting with us the whole time. My mind clicked back to Augusta's behavior since we arrived at Fortnum & Mason. Come to think of it, she *had* made a trip to the ladies' room before we sat down. I figured she wanted to freshen up after her fainting spell. But could she have given the note to the waiter and asked him to place it under the scone?

I handed the note to Bess and Augusta, who were sitting next to each other. "Who put this under your scone, Nancy?" Bess asked as she scanned the message.

Augusta seemed just as surprised as Bess. "Weird!" she exclaimed. "Is someone after you or something, Nancy?"

I studied her face, which mixed surprise, confusion, and amusement, as if she thought the note might be a silly trick. Guilt was nowhere to be seen. Maybe she was just a really good actress. Being in the theater, she'd have lots of opportunities to observe skilled actors, wouldn't she?

I glanced back at the note. "It says I need to be at this store at the end of the day. Augusta, do you know what time the sun sets here?" I couldn't remember anything from the day before. It was one big blur after Dad went missing.

Augusta frowned. "Sunset would be between eight and nine p.m., I believe. I can't tell you exactly, Nancy, but in May the sun won't set for a while because we're so far north. Winter is another story, though. Then the sun sets in the middle of the afternoon."

"So if we get to the store between eight and nine, that should do it?" Bess asked.

"I'd say so," Augusta said. "What a thoroughly odd note. Do you girls have any idea what it could possibly be about?"

"No," I said. "But I'm curious to find out more about this store."

"Well, be careful," Augusta warned. "You have almost three hours to change your mind about going there. I hope you don't go. It sounds dangerous."

I checked my watch. A wave of cold, like ice water, washed through me. It was nearly five o'clock and no really good clues on Dad had come our way since he disappeared. He'd been missing for almost a whole day! He could be anywhere, in any situation. Though probably a bad one since kidnapped people usually don't get the red-carpet treatment. Maybe the police would have good news by now. I longed to call them, but I didn't want Augusta to know more about me than I could help. Despite her show of innocence, she was still a suspect.

Where could Dad be? My anxiety about him was blasting through me like an air conditioner, chilling my thoughts. But I had to think straight for Dad's sake. Wherever he was, he depended on me. Still, keeping a grip on my emotions was incredibly hard. I mean, I had no idea if he was even okay.

I forced myself to put those thoughts aside. Remembering Augusta's visit to Books of Olde, I said, "Speaking of stores, do you know a bookstore called Books of Olde? It sells inexpensive copies of Shakespeare's plays."

"And expensive ones!" Augusta cried. "Sure, I know that store. It's in my neighborhood. It sells used books cheaply and rare ones for a price. Anyway, the old man who owns it is a sweetheart."

"Have you ever noticed a middle-aged man in there with brown hair graying around the temples? Or a heavyset woman with red cheeks who wears her gray hair in a bun?" I asked, trying to connect the store with the Elliotts.

"Can't say I have," Augusta said, "though I don't pay much attention to other customers while I'm browsing there." As she spoke, Augusta was finishing her meal. She seemed kind of restless, but I had to ask her more questions about her connection to Dr. Burnham before she left.

"So you have no idea how your manuscript got on Dr. Burnham's floor?" I asked.

"None at all," she said briskly. "He was my professor at the university five years ago."

"Have you had contact with him since?" I pressed.

"Nancy," Augusta said with a hint of annoyance, "I've got to go. Let's get the check. As promised, this is my treat."

She barely spoke to us as she asked for the check and paid the bill. The subject of Dr. Burnham had made her clam up. My detective sense told me that Augusta had something to hide. I intended to find out what that was.

On our way out, I found our waiter clearing

dishes in a corner. I lingered for a moment to chat with him. "Excuse me," I said, "did you see anyone put a note under my scone?"

He peered at me in surprise. "If I'd seen someone tamper with your food, I never would have served it to you."

"Was my plate ever unattended?" I asked.

"Yes, for about thirty seconds while I served someone else. It was on a rack near the entrance to the room."

Hmm. So someone from the outside could have sneaked the note under my scone then. If the waiter was telling me the truth, then Augusta must be innocent because she'd been with us while the scones were waiting. But what if Augusta had bribed the waiter to place the note?

I thanked him, then joined Bess and Augusta up on the street. "Well, girls, it's been nice meeting you," Augusta said. "Have a wonderful time in London, and don't forget to attend *Romeo and Juliet* tomorrow evening."

"We'd never miss that!" Bess exclaimed. "It sounds awesome."

We thanked Augusta again for the tickets. After she left, I turned to Bess and said, "Let's find a pay phone and check in with the police."

Five minutes later I hung up a nearby phone, disappointed. The police hadn't found Dad, or any clues to his whereabouts. They'd found no signs of the Elliotts, either. "Rest assured that an all points bulletin has been issued for them, Nancy," Constable Reynolds had declared.

Time to check in with Dr. Burnham. I would have called him first thing this morning to tell him about Dad, but the time difference meant that he would have been asleep. Now it was midmorning for him. I crossed my fingers that he'd be home and not teaching.

He answered my call on the second ring, and I immediately told him about Dad. "What?" he cried, sounding stunned. "Nancy, are you sure?"

"Unfortunately, yes. There was a struggle in his room, and he never came back last night."

After a few seconds of silence, Dr. Burnham muttered, "I sure hope the police are doing their job."

"Dr. Burnham, I need to ask you a couple of questions. Have you ever heard of Books of Olde? Or Augusta Dorrance?"

"No to the first question. Yes to the second," Dr. Burnham replied. An edge crept into his voice as he explained, "Augusta used to be a student of mine. She's a playwright now, and I haven't seen her in years. Nancy, I'm glad you called me, because I was going to call you. I'm leaving for England tomorrow night to deal with this mess about my house. I finally found a substitute teacher for my classes."

"That's great, Dr. Burnham," I said. "I look forward to seeing you. I hope I'll have your mystery solved by then. And I really hope I'll find my father."

After we hung up, Bess suggested swinging by Dr. Burnham's house. "Maybe we should check it to make sure we didn't miss any clues."

"Well, we haven't checked the Elliotts' flat yet," I said. "Why don't we make sure the police didn't overlook anything there? Constable Reynolds gave me their address, and we've got time."

Twenty minutes later we nodded hello to the constable on duty at the Elliotts' flat, which was on the ground floor of a narrow row house in East London. The furniture inside was sparse and plain, and the closets, file cabinets, and dressers had only a few random things in them. No clues. No sign that Dad had ever been there at all.

The rays of the lowering sun glanced across my eyes as I scanned the backyard garden. A wave of impatience washed over me. The day was slipping away, minute by minute, and what real clues had I found that would help me locate Dad? Meanwhile he was waiting somewhere, confident that my detective skills would be up to the search. I had to find him soon!

I turned to Bess. "This place is a bust, and the police have it covered anyway, in case the Elliotts return. You know what I'd like to do? Get to that store, Todd, and interview the owner."

"But you're not supposed to be there till sunset, Nancy," Bess countered. "We've still got a little while until the sun's last ray, or whatever the poem said."

"Yeah, but if I follow those instructions exactly, I'll fall into this person's plans and end up a step behind. I need to take control of things. If there's anything suspicious going on at that store, now is the time to check it out, when no one expects us."

"Okay," Bess said. "Then how do we get there?"

I dug out my guidebook, which told us that during the sixties, when the Beatles were taking the world by storm and London was super trendy, Carnaby Street ruled the fashion world. After some hard times in between, the street was making a comeback. So when Bess and I got off the Tube at Oxford Circus near Carnaby Street, we weren't surprised to see several cool clothing stores scattered around. And once we'd turned the corner and found Todd—a hushed place with beige as its theme color—we weren't surprised to see hip clothes from the latest designers hanging elegantly on the racks.

But the next sight was a shocker. A tall man with dreadlocks emerged from behind the counter and smiled. "May I help you, ladies?" he asked. It was Augusta's friend!

10

Locked In

I did a double take.

"Is something wrong?" the man asked, his smile changing quickly to a frown.

"Uh, no," I stammered. "It's just that we saw you earlier today, so we're kind of surprised to run into you here. Are you a friend of Augusta's? I'm Nancy Drew and this is my friend Bess Marvin."

The man smiled again as he shook our hands. "So nice to meet you girls," he said in a West Indian accent. "I'm Duncan Smithson. I'm actually a reggae singer in the play Augusta directed."

"Really? The last time I checked, there's no part for a reggae singer in *Romeo and Juliet*," Bess said.

Duncan laughed. "In Augusta's version of it, there

is. See, I play the part of Friar Laurence, and Augusta has me singing my lines."

"That is so cool," Bess declared. "I can't wait to see you perform tomorrow night. Augusta gave us complimentary tickets. But if you're an actor in the play, why are you working here?"

"Living in London is expensive," Duncan explained. "I work here in my spare time to put some money in the bank. But now it's my turn to ask you girls some questions. Where did you see me with Augusta?"

"On the boat to the Tower," I said.

"You were there?" Duncan said, looking pleased. "Wasn't it a lovely day on the river?" Before I could answer, Duncan went on, "You see, I'd never been to the Tower, so Augusta invited me to join her for a quick tour of it. I'm glad I did. I got a fabulous overview of English history."

"Did you leave the Tower early? We stopped seeing you," I said.

"I had to open the store," Duncan replied. "Our hours here are from one to nine." As I opened my mouth to ask him more questions, Duncan held up his hand. "Wait. I believe it's my turn to ask you a question. How do you girls know Augusta?"

"Just by being tourists together," I explained. "We were in the same car on the London Eye, and afterward we all got hungry and went out for tea." I decided not to mention Augusta's fainting spell. It didn't seem that relevant, and she might consider it embarrassing. I paused. My next question needed some tact. I shot Duncan a smile. "My turn for a question, right? I need your opinion on something. The name Samuel Burnham. Does it ring a bell?"

Duncan gaped. "Samuel Burnham? Did you mention him to Augusta?"

"Yes, and the moment I said his name, Augusta clammed up. She'd been really friendly and talkative with us up until then. Do you know why she would have had such a weird reaction?"

Duncan put up his hand. "Wait! My turn. Why did you mention Dr. Burnham to Augusta? Do you know him?"

"Yes. He's teaching at my friend's college in America on exchange from the University of London. When Augusta told us that she'd been a student at the university, I thought she might know him."

"Samuel Burnham," Duncan said thoughtfully. "He's the chap who sued Augusta for plagiarism. No wonder she had a negative reaction."

Bess and I exchanged looks. A lawsuit! If Dr. Burnham had sued Augusta for plagiarism, she probably wouldn't like him very much. Which means she'd have a motive for stealing his stuff.

"Who won the lawsuit?" I asked.

"Dr. Burnham," Duncan said. "Augusta was pretty upset at losing, especially because he was her former professor and she respected him. You see, his work totally inspired her, and she felt that her work honored his because it had a similar style. But she never deliberately stole his ideas." Duncan shrugged. "Although the judge didn't see things that way."

"Did this happen recently?" I asked.

"A couple of years ago," Duncan replied. "Anyway, it was a big deal for Augusta."

"Is she still angry about it?" Bess asked.

"She feels betrayed," Duncan said. "Naturally. Wouldn't you?"

"But she's had a lot of success anyway," I pointed out.

Duncan frowned. "As a director, yes, but she's still a struggling playwright. The publication of her first play was stopped because of the lawsuit, so she couldn't have it performed. She hopes she'll have better luck with the one she's just finished."

"Is that *The Scottish Play*?" I asked. "She was telling us about it at tea."

Duncan nodded, holding up crossed fingers. "I sure hope it works out for her. She's a hard worker and deserves some luck."

I chewed my lip, thinking. Why had that play been

tossed on Dr. Burnham's floor? There was something between Dr. Burnham and Augusta that I wasn't quite getting. One thing was clear: Augusta held a grudge against him. She had a motive to hurt him. In my opinion, when someone cooks up a crime, motive is the basic ingredient, with a dash of means and opportunity thrown in for spice.

Duncan's answers were intriguing, but what did they have to do with Dad? No matter how hard I tried, I couldn't come up with an answer. All I knew was that the person who took him had dropped a rare-book seller's address on the hotel floor the same evening that rare books had been stolen from Dr. Burnham. And Augusta had a motive for hurting Dr. Burnham, and she was a frequent customer at Books of Olde. Meanwhile the Elliotts, who had been sneaking around Dr. Burnham's house just before the theft, had completely disappeared.

I glanced outside. The sun was a sinking flame in the sky, shooting pink streaks into a lavender backdrop like a fireworks sparkler. Sunset was moments away.

"So what brings you to Todd, girls?" Duncan asked, breaking into my thoughts. "A little shopping spree? Some fashionable clothes to buy as trip souvenirs?"

I fished the poem from my pocket and handed it

to Duncan. "This note led us here," I told him. "Do you have any idea who could have sent it to me?"

Duncan's hand shook as he read the note. "What kind of weirdo wrote this?" he asked, outraged. "I don't want to scare you girls, but it sounds like someone really has it in for you. Did this note come to you in the mail?"

"Sort of," I fudged, not wanting to give him too much information. I studied him, trying to figure out how clueless he really was about the note. I reminded myself that he was an accomplished actor.

"So who owns this store?" Bess asked, looking around at the sleek outfits draped over mannequins that were posed dramatically around the room.

"A young woman named Todd," Duncan replied, "with a gift for fashion."

"Todd is a woman?" Bess asked. "Well, I guess I shouldn't be so surprised. Our best friend is named George, and she's a girl."

Duncan chuckled. "Eustacia Todd Elliott is her name. She never liked her first name, Eustacia."

Who cared about first or middle names—it was her last name that grabbed my attention! "You say Todd's last name is Elliott?" I asked. "Is she any relation to the Mr. and Mrs. Elliott in Knightsbridge?"

Duncan's eyes locked with mine. "It's a common last name, Nancy. Can you give me more details?"

"The Elliotts are middle aged. Mr. Elliott is a retired security guard and Mrs. Elliott's a housekeeper. He's kind of thin with brownish gray hair, and she's plump with gray hair and rosy cheeks."

Duncan looked shocked. "You're describing her parents. How do you know them?"

"Mrs. Elliott is Dr. Burnham's housekeeper." Not wanting to give out too much information, I quickly added, "Have you seen the Elliotts around lately?"

Duncan's lip curled in contempt. "Todd is estranged from her parents, and I haven't seen them in months."

"Has anyone been nosing around the store?" I asked. "I mean, in a suspicious way?"

Duncan flinched, as if I'd somehow hurled an insult at him. "Why would I allow anyone to lurk around the store?" he said indignantly. "If either Todd or I saw a shifty-looking person hanging around, we'd bust them for sure."

"The person who wants to meet here at sunset sounds kind of shifty," I said.

Duncan nodded gravely. "He, or she, sounds very odd. Girls, you're welcome to wait around here till sunset and see what happens. As I mentioned, the store doesn't close till nine o'clock."

At that moment a young woman wearing a miniskirt entered the store. Flicking back her long chestnut brown hair, she haughtily scanned the merchandise. Bess elbowed me. "Do you think that's the note writer?" she whispered.

"I can't tell," I murmured back. We watched the woman flip through some dresses on a rack and casually remove two of them. Bringing them over to Duncan, she held a sleeveless scarlet and emerald silk dress up to her chest.

"What do you think of this?" she asked him. "I need a nice dress to wear to an art benefit next week. Or this." She replaced it with a black velvet cocktail dress glittering with rhinestones on the waist and chest. "I can't decide."

"I like the first dress," Bess said firmly. "The black one looks too hot for this weather." In a low voice, she added to me, "She's only a shopper. It's obvious now."

"Hang on a sec," Duncan said to the shopper, "let me show you this slinky mauve chiffon that would really flatter your hair." He hurried toward a rack in the far corner.

While Duncan was distracted by the shopper, I got distracted by a white rectangular object lying on his chair. Curious, I stepped behind the counter and sneaked a glance. It was an appointment book with Duncan's name on it and looked as if it might have a few juicy secrets to reveal. I shot a glance at

Duncan—he was still with the shopper. Finally, an opportunity to snoop!

I picked up the book. Today's space was blank, but tomorrow's had an interesting notation: *X is coming to Globe at intermission. Meet by backstage entrance. Must give cash.* There was also a line drawn through the week ending today, with a scrawl that said, *T. away in France. Must work more hours!*

"I'm going to think about it," the woman announced, handing Duncan a pile of dresses. "I'll come back if I'm interested." As she moved toward the door, I set Duncan's book back down on the chair.

"Hey, Duncan," I asked, "is Todd around?"

"She's been away this week, but she'll be back tomorrow."

"Who minds the shop while you perform?" Bess asked.

"No one. When I perform, I have to close it. I have no choice, since Todd and I are the only shop-keepers here."

"Doesn't your business suffer when you close during regular hours?" Bess asked.

Duncan shrugged. "Todd went to Paris to buy for the store, and that's an important trip for the business. The store will come out ahead in the long run, even if I have to close it a couple times. I usually hang a little sign on the front door, so people will know to come back at a different hour."

"Do you know whether the Elliotts have another home besides their London flat?" I asked.

"They do indeed—a small country cottage near Stonehenge." He scrawled an address on a yellow Post-it and handed it to me.

"Thanks!" I said excitedly. What a break! For the first time I had a clue about where to look for Dad.

A blaze of sunlight shot through the front window of the store, briefly turning the cool beige interior a hot magenta. I glanced outside just in time to see the sun making a fiery descent below the London skyline, dazzling the black rooftops with one last burst of energy. I checked my watch. It was already after eight!

"This person is late!" Bess declared. "That was definitely the sun's last ray."

"Let's just wait a while longer," I said. But as each minute ticked by, my hope began to fade.

Bess and I waited until the sky was as dark as London ever gets, with millions of electric lights casting a hazy glow over it. Meanwhile Duncan helped a few new customers before each one walked out, dashing our hopes. Finally Duncan began switching off lights. "Girls, I'm afraid it's closing time. Too bad no one ever came."

"But why would someone bring us here on a wild-goose chase?" Bess asked, her voice tinged with disappointment.

"I don't know," I said, baffled. Still, I was glad we'd come. At least I had a better idea of where to look for the Elliotts. And a new person to check out—"X."

Back at the hotel I immediately called the police to give them the Elliotts' Stonehenge address. "Sorry to disappoint you, Nancy," Constable Reynolds said over the phone. "But the landlady already gave us their country address. The local police checked it and found no sign of the Elliotts—or your father."

The news from the American Embassy was no better. "We're working closely with the London police, Ms. Drew," an official there told me when I called. "We're doing our best."

Everyone was doing their best, including me, but it wasn't good enough. My heart sank, and my brain felt numb. There was no guarantee my detective skills would work this time. Try as I might to find him, Dad seemed to have disappeared off the face of the earth.

Thanks to the hot night—and the fact that air-conditioning was rare in English hotels—I slipped on a tank top and pajama shorts and climbed into bed as Bess showered. Discouraged and terrified for Dad, I drifted into sleep, remembering at the last second that we'd never even had dinner.

. . .

"Nancy, wake up!" Bess said, smiling down at me as she wheeled a room-service tray between our beds. I smelled scrambled eggs and bacon. Was it morning already? I sat up in bed, my stomach growling, and saw that Bess had pulled the curtains open to reveal another sunny day.

"I ordered us a big breakfast to make up for missing dinner last night," Bess said brightly. "We need every ounce of energy for our search!"

"Thanks, Bess," I said. "You're the best."

"I've even checked in with Constable Reynolds," she said. "Does the man ever sleep? He seems to be chained to his desk. Unfortunately, he didn't have any news for us."

Her words cut through my grogginess, and a burst of adrenaline shot me out of bed. I showered, dressed, and ate a hearty breakfast. As Bess had said, we needed all our energy for the search.

"I just wonder where Dad could be," I said. I sat down on the edge of my bed to think. "I can't help wondering whether he's hurt."

"I know how horrible you must feel, Nancy," Bess said sympathetically. "But those thoughts will drive you crazy. Let's just do our best to concentrate on the case, one clue at a time. Now that you've got some food inside you, let's review our leads."

I tried to focus. Dad was depending on my brain to function normally. And Bess was right—we had to go through our leads, one by one. "Well," I began, "I've got the address of Books of Olde that was dropped by the person who took Dad. Then Augusta, whose manuscript had been left at Dr. Burnham's house, turned up at Books of Olde. She was looking for a used copy of *Macbeth*, but the owner only had a rare one that Augusta couldn't afford."

"But he didn't have a rare copy of *King Lear*," Bess said, "even though one had been stolen from Dr. Burnham's house."

"Also, Dr. Burnham used to be Augusta's professor, but she had no clue how her manuscript ended up on his floor."

"She seemed really freaked by that," Bess added. "What else? Oh, yes—that warning at the Tower when Augusta was nearby. Remember, it was a woman pretending to be a ghost."

"She knew our names, too. And Bess, let's not forget about Dr. Burnham's lawsuit. He'd sued Augusta for plagiarism—and won!"

"That's huge," Bess said. "And what about the note luring us to Todd? Why didn't anyone show up there at sunset? And don't you think it's weird that Duncan is the shopkeeper and he's Augusta's friend? That's just too coincidental in my opinion. Also, the store belongs to the Elliotts' daughter, who's away. How does that puzzle piece fit?"

I sifted every tiny detail of the case through my mind. "Oh, Bess, I forgot to tell you!" I cried. "Duncan is meeting someone at the theater tonight. Someone he owes money to."

Bess raised her eyebrows. "How do you think these leads all work together, Nancy?"

My head was spinning. "I don't know, but there's an answer somewhere. I think we should try a different angle and talk to some of Dr. Burnham's colleagues at the University of London. Someone there might be able to tell us if he has any enemies."

"Good idea. And maybe someone will remember Augusta from her student days and give us some helpful hints about her."

I gave Bess the thumbs-up sign, and then we got ready to go.

A half hour later Bess and I stood outside the university, frowning at a locked entrance.

"How could I be so clueless, Bess? It's Sunday!" I cried, jiggling the lock. I quickly gave up. Even if I could get in the door, Dr. Burnham's colleagues wouldn't be there.

"Nancy, be fair to yourself," Bess said, patting me on the back. "You've had a lot on your mind lately."

Bess was right. Between the time change from America to England, and then freaking out about Dad, I'd totally forgotten what day it was. I had to calm down and think.

An idea flashed into my mind. "Bess, the British Museum is nearby. I noticed it as we were walking here. Wasn't Mr. Elliott a security guard there once?"

"That's what Constable Reynolds told us," Bess said. "Maybe some of the employees can tell us more about him."

"Let's head over there now."

Once inside the museum, Bess and I were directed to two older security guards who might remember Mr. Elliott. Bess headed to the guard near an upstairs entrance, while I searched for one posted in a large room nearby.

The room I entered was filled with mummies, but there was no live person in sight. Maybe the guard was around a corner. "Hello?" I called. But the only voice I heard was my own, echoing off the walls.

A large closetlike space opened on my left. I peeked inside at a mummy on a dais. Stepping in, I scanned the area behind the mummy for the guard.

The door slammed shut. I whirled around. No

one was there. Rushing back to the door, I pushed on it hard, but it wouldn't budge. I was locked in with the mummy! "Bess," I shouted. "I'm stuck in here!"

Bess's voice, floating through the thick door, sounded far away, as if it was underwater. "Nancy, help me!" she cried.

11

Upstaged

Bess!" I yelled. "Are you okay?" I had to get out
of there to rescue her! But how? I shouted again for
help. No answer. My heart sank. It was still pretty
early on a Sunday morning, and visitors had been
scarce when we came in. My mind clicked back to
three minutes ago and brought up an image I didn't
want to see. I'd been the only person in that big
mummy room. Sooner or later, a guard was sure to
come by and hear me, but in time to rescue Bess?

I pushed on the door again. "Help!" I cried. The
door handle clicked. I held my breath. Who was out
there? The person who had locked me in? I couldn't
do anything except hope that wasn't true. "I'm in
here!" I yelled, pushing the door with my shoulder.

The door opened, and I fell into my rescuer's arms. Bess!

"Nancy, are you all right?" she asked breathlessly.

"I'm fine, Bess, but how are you? I thought you were in trouble."

"Don't worry about me. I'm okay." Gasping for air, with her hair all mussed, Bess did not look okay.

"Tell me what happened," I urged.

"I heard a door slam shut, and when I went to investigate, someone grabbed me from behind in a neck lock," Bess explained. "I think it was a man, because the arm felt muscular inside his leather jacket."

"Did he say anything?"

"Not a word, not even when I scratched at his hand. I must have hit a sensitive spot because he pushed me onto the floor and ran away."

"Bess, are you sure you aren't hurt?"

Bess grinned. "Hey, I got off easy, Nancy. You were locked in a closet with a mummy!"

I laughed. "One thing's for sure," I added. "If Augusta is guilty, she has a guy helping her."

We asked the security guard in the hall whether he'd seen a man in a leather jacket leaving the museum. "At this hour," he replied, "I usually see people *coming in* to the museum. But wait! I believe I did see someone leave, a tall gentleman with dreadlocks. And yes, he was dressed in black leather."

Bess and I traded alarmed looks. Duncan Smithson? I asked the guard, "Do you remember someone named Mr. Elliott who worked here a few years back?"

"Nope, the name doesn't ring a bell at all," the guard said. "Sorry, miss."

We also struck out with the other older guard, once we'd found him. He didn't remember Mr. Elliott either. On the stairs outside the museum, Bess and I discussed our options.

"I think we should go to Todd and confront Duncan," I said. "I mean, he attacked you and locked me in!"

"But, Nancy, we can't be sure it was Duncan," Bess said. "Also, Todd doesn't even open till one o'clock. And Duncan may not go there at all today. He's performing later! Anyway, we'll see him at the play. Let's question him then."

Bess was right. My anxiety about Dad was making me too emotional. I had to calm down so I could think as logically as I normally do. Anyway, I hadn't forgotten Duncan's note in his book about meeting X at intermission. I intended to get to the bottom of that, or my name isn't Nancy Drew. "Okay, Bess, then let's take the Tube to Dr. Burnham's house. I want to make sure we haven't missed any clues there."

• • •

Stationed by the front door at Dr. Burnham's was a young, eager-looking constable with bright brown eyes. Bess and I smiled at him as we climbed up the portico steps.

"I'm Nancy Drew," I said, introducing myself, "and this is my friend Bess Marvin. We're helping the police with Dr. Burnham's case."

"Ah, yes, of course! Ms. Drew and Ms. Marvin," he said pleasantly. "I recognize your names. Please, girls, go right on in." He unlocked the front door for us and waved us inside. After thanking him, Bess and I fanned out across the house, looking for missed clues.

"I'll take the upstairs," I suggested.

"Okay, then I'll prowl around down here," Bess said.

Upstairs, four bedrooms opened off a wide front hall. Whichever room the Elliotts had used would probably be the best one for clues. Who knew what evidence they'd left in their hurry to quit the scene of the crime? An accomplice's address? Someone's name? But all the rooms were so tidy that they reminded me more of hotel rooms than a house. Either Dr. Burnham was a total neat freak, or the Elliotts had made sure to leave no hints about themselves. Most of the closets or drawers were bare, except for a few clothes stashed here and there. From the sizes of the suits and jackets, I guessed they belonged to Dr. Burnham.

The biggest bedroom had a double bed, a plain brown carpet, and a dresser. Nothing fancy. On the bedside table, a man and woman smiled out from a leather picture frame—Dr. Burnham's parents, maybe? A dog-eared paperback dictionary lay beside the photo. Those things made me think this room was Dr. Burnham's.

I tugged on the table's one drawer. It wouldn't budge. Either the heat was making it stick, or it was locked. And if it was locked, what was inside it that someone didn't want seen?

Only one way to find out. If it was stuck, my skill with the barrette would be useless. If it was locked, my barrette would take care of that problem pronto.

I unclipped my ponytail and got to work. Within seconds of jiggling the lock, the drawer sprang open.

"Wow, Nancy, you sure didn't waste any time picking that lock," Bess said as she approached me from behind.

"It's a specialty of mine," I said, shooting her a grin over my shoulder. I glanced back at the drawer, where a phone book and several wadded receipts had been stuffed inside.

"By the way," Bess said, "I found nothing down-stairs. Everything looks too neat, not great for clues. If you ask me, this place is more like a showroom than a house. But who wants to live in a show-room?"

"The Elliotts must have straightened up before they left. Anyway, this drawer looks promising with all these messy papers. I'll check them out, but first let's see what's under this phone book." I lifted it out—and did a double take. A leather volume with gold lettering that spelled the words "King Lear" lay inside the drawer.

I took it out and inspected the cover, made of a deep red morocco leather that had been lovingly cared for with some sort of oil, probably to preserve it. The edges of the pages had been tinted with gold leaf, and the pages themselves were thin, a little yellowed, and rough. I met Bess's gaze, and I knew she shared my thoughts. Could this be Dr. Burnham's rare copy of *King Lear*?

I carefully opened the book to the title page. Words in old-fashioned lettering popped up at me:

M. William Shak-speare:
HIS
True Chronicle Historie of the life and
death of King Lear and his three Daughters.

It continued a bit more, but I got the gist.

"Did Dr. Burnham just forget it was in here?" I

mused as I put the book back and locked the drawer.

"Or maybe it's a different edition," Bess suggested. "Old but not as rare as the one that was stolen."

"Maybe," I said thoughtfully. "But why would he keep it in a locked drawer? Anyway, Dr. Burnham's plane arrives tomorrow morning. We can ask him then. Meanwhile, it's already midafternoon. Let's grab lunch and then head over to the Globe Theatre for the performance. I don't want to be late for Duncan and X's big meeting."

Bess and I ate lunch at an Indian restaurant in Notting Hill, a lively part of London popular with immigrants, artists, and trendy young people. I knew the tandoori chicken with mango chutney would normally be delicious, but I couldn't enjoy anything with Dad still missing. Earlier, at the museum and at Dr. Burnham's house, when I was focused on clues and suspects, I'd felt better, but during breaks from the case like now, anxious thoughts crowded my mind. I needed to feel I was doing something to solve the case. But I felt really frustrated with it. Dad had been gone for two days! Where were the Elliotts? And how did the burglary at Dr. Burnham's house relate to Dad?

"I know you're feeling awful, Nancy," Bess said, sensing my thoughts. "But we'll find your dad, I know it."

"Thanks, Bess," I said as we paid our lunch bill.

"What's keeping me going now is the one lead we've got left—Duncan and his meeting with X at the Globe."

An hour later Bess and I were sitting at the Globe Theatre, waiting for *Romeo and Juliet* to begin. "This place is awesome," Bess commented, marveling at the open-air replica of Shakespeare's famous original theater with its colorfully painted stage set. "And the theater is packed."

That included the standing-room area around the stage for hundreds of spectators who couldn't get a seat, just as in Shakespeare's time. I'd read in my guidebook that the artistic director of the theater wanted the new Globe to be totally faithful to the original. He even mentioned that he'd be happy if the audience threw fruit at the actors as the Elizabethans did.

Bess elbowed me. "Hey, Nancy, isn't that Daniela Ramirez? The girl we met yesterday on the London Eye?"

I followed Bess's gaze. Sure enough, a young girl with long dark hair was hurrying to take her seat. The bridesmaid from yesterday's wedding, Daniela! Since we were seated next to an aisle, it was easy for me to stand up and greet her.

"Nancy Drew! And Bess Marvin!" Daniela

exclaimed as Bess and I reintroduced ourselves. "What a small world."

"Are you looking forward to the play, Daniela?" I asked her.

"I sure am. *Romeo and Juliet* is my favorite Shakespeare tragedy, but I think his comedies are awesome."

"I totally agree," Bess said brightly. "Anyway, even though it's sad, there's plenty of comedy in *Romeo and Juliet*, and it's so romantic! You must be a precocious reader, Daniela."

"I just really like to read," Daniela replied modestly as her mother waved her along. "Anyway, I'd better find my seat. It was nice seeing you two. Enjoy the play!"

I wanted to tell Daniela that Augusta Dorrance, whom Daniela had met yesterday, was the director of this play, but there wasn't enough time. Less than a minute later, an actor wearing black jeans and a T-shirt strode onto the stage and began to recite the famous opening lines of the play: "Two households, both alike in dignity, / In fair Verona, where we lay our scene, / From ancient grudge break to new mutiny, / Where civil blood makes civil hands unclean...."

I leaned forward, eager for the moment when Friar Laurence would appear. Meanwhile Augusta's adaptation of *Romeo and Juliet* held the audience in a sort of magic spell as people alternately laughed, gasped, and sighed. In her version, Romeo and Juliet were modern London teens, children of opposing Parliament members, Labor and Conservative. After a few scenes went by, guitar notes and drumbeats suddenly filled the air, and Duncan rushed onto the stage dressed as the friar and singing his lines. "The gray-eyed morn smiles on the frowning night, / Check'ring the eastern clouds with streaks of light . . . ," he sang in a booming baritone to a reggae beat.

The moment I heard him, my mind went into overdrive. How could Bess and I get backstage to spy on Duncan's meeting with X? Leaning toward me, Bess whispered, "At first I thought a singing friar might be kind of lame, but he's really good!"

Duncan *was* good, but I still couldn't concentrate on the play. Every moment we weren't actively searching for Dad seemed like a waste.

Finally, intermission! The moment the characters left the stage, I hopped out of my seat. "Bess, I don't want to miss Duncan and X. We've got to find the backstage entrance!"

Bess and I wove our way between wandering audience members and found a backstage entrance. "Maybe we can sneak in while no one is looking," I said.

Thanks to the huge crowd of theatergoers and

busy props people bustling around, we slid through the opening undetected. "Mission accomplished," I said, feeling satisfied. "Now, where are we going to hide so we can spy on Duncan?"

I scanned the area, which was separated from the stage by a small side curtain masking part of the set. But if we hid behind the curtain, we'd be on the stage. If only there was a closet or some props that we could hide behind, but the only objects near us were several medium-size boxes filled with clothes, all too small for us to fit inside. I suddenly felt very exposed. Duncan would recognize us instantly and suspect we were spying on him.

"Nancy!" Bess cried. "I have an idea." Holding up some of the clothes from the boxes, she went on, "Remember, Juliet's friends at her parents' feast were wearing these costumes? Maybe if we put them on, we'll blend in with the real actors."

"Brilliant, Bess!" I flashed her a grateful smile. "I'm counting on you to help me think while my mind is so muddled about Dad. I just hope the real actors don't come along and suddenly need their costumes."

Around the corner from the backstage entrance was a small dressing room where we quickly changed into the black miniskirts, pink tank tops, and flip-flops that Juliet's friends had been wearing.

"Nancy, you look exactly like that strawberry blond actress, the one Juliet's father urged onto the dance floor," Bess said, giggling as we emerged from the room. "No one will ever think we're imposters."

A props person dashed by us, along with a couple of actors, but they didn't give us a second glance. "We might have to test our acting skills before this is all over," I said.

"Oh, I think we're up to it," Bess said, squaring her shoulders.

A familiar figure, milling around the backstage entrance, grabbed my attention. "Look, Bess, there's Duncan. In a moment, we'll know X's identity!" Duncan scowled impatiently as he checked his watch. "Let's hang out nearby," I whispered. "We can pretend we're talking about the play."

But minutes passed with no X in sight. The lights blinked, signaling the end of intermission. I sighed. Duncan wasn't the only impatient person around. "Where could X be?" I murmured, as Duncan kept pacing the floor.

The lights blinked again, and Duncan groaned in frustration. "Should we go back to our seats?" Bess wondered. I looked toward the side curtain separating us from the stage and the audience beyond it. By now the audience was already completely quiet.

A hand shoved me from behind. Someone was

pushing us through the side curtain and onto the stage!

Bess and I traded shocked looks. Before our astonished eyes was an audience of hundreds, all expecting us to say something. I held my breath, hoping they wouldn't throw any fruit!

12

Showdown

An awkward hush filled the theater, and my legs felt like Jell-O. How much longer would they hold me up? Just as I thought I'd collapse, drumbeats rolled and guitar chords twanged as a familiar voice approached us from behind, singing, "So smile the heavens upon this holy act / That after-hours with sorrow chide us not!"

I couldn't believe our luck! Duncan's appearance had saved us from total embarrassment—at least so far. And when he was followed onstage by Romeo and then Juliet, speaking their lines, I knew that Bess and I were just part of the backdrop. Soon the scene ended, and Duncan, linking arms, escorted Bess and me backstage. In a seamless switch, we were replaced onstage by a group of Romeo's friends.

"So we meet again," Duncan snarled. "I think we need to have a little talk, ladies."

Shoving us into the dressing room where Bess and I had changed, he shut the door and stood before it, his arms crossed. His friar's costume couldn't mask his muscular six-foot frame, which towered over us. "Why are you girls stalking me?" he blurted out. "I'm an honest chap, and I expect the same of others. So you need to level with me. Now."

"What makes you think we're stalking you?" I asked.

Duncan snorted. "I'm not an idiot. I saw you lurking by the entrance near me. I think you sneaked a look at my date book yesterday, saw my note, and decided to spy on me. Your costumes didn't fool me for a second. In fact, I was the one who pushed you onto the stage to teach you a lesson—not to interfere!"

"What!" Bess exclaimed. "So we weren't even supposed to be in that act? Won't you get in trouble for doing that?"

Duncan shrugged. "Augusta had been considering using some of the minor characters as a backdrop in certain scenes, kind of like a Greek chorus, to remind viewers that Romeo and Juliet's lives had been fated by their warring families. Your appearance could be considered a trial run."

117

"In front of a live audience?" I asked, shocked.

Duncan's eyes flashed. "I was very angry at you. I acted without thinking. So sue me. Anyway, you haven't answered my question."

I thought about fudging my answer, but Duncan was a whole lot bigger than I was. He might be a hothead, but he wasn't stupid. "You're right, Duncan," I said, "Bess and I were spying on you. See, my dad was kidnapped two nights ago, and Bess and I have been looking for him nonstop. We think his disappearance has something to do with a burglary at Dr. Burnham's house. Augusta was a suspect, so that made you one too since you guys spent so much time together yesterday. Plus, the note I got at Fortnum and Mason led me to your store."

"I don't care how suspicious I seemed," he growled. "You read private entries in my date book."

"But if your dad were missing, you'd investigate every lead you possibly could. Plus, we have reason to believe that you attacked us at the British Museum earlier today." The moment those words escaped my mouth, Bess nudged me. Whoops. Maybe that wasn't the wisest thing to say when we were alone in a room with him.

Duncan shook with fury. "I was nowhere near the museum today!" he spat. "Todd returned from France this morning. She can vouch for me. We worked together at the store before it opened, cataloging new inventory. I came directly here in the afternoon. What gave you the insane idea that I attacked you?"

"A guard described you," I replied. "Obviously, he was wrong."

"Anyway, who is X?" Bess asked, changing the subject.

Taking a deep breath, Duncan said, "A friend of mine named Xavier. I bought a guitar from him last week, and he was supposed to come to the performance today to collect his cash. I guess he'll track me down after the play is over."

I checked my watch. Eight o'clock. Todd would probably still be at her store. I could check Duncan's story with her and maybe find out where her parents were. That information could lead me to Dad.

I shot a look at Duncan. Should I believe him? The museum guard described him as Bess's attacker, yet Duncan vowed he had an alibi. I'd know the answer to that question soon enough, but one thing was clear. No way could I sit through the rest of this play when Todd was just a cab ride away.

Duncan frowned. "So why do you suspect Augusta?" he asked.

"You said yourself that she's angry at Dr. Burnham," I explained. "She holds a grudge from that lawsuit."

"Not enough to burglarize his house!"

"But the manuscript for her new play was found on the floor of his house right after it had been burglarized," I announced.

"That doesn't mean she was the thief. She would never steal Dr. Burnham's stuff just because she's mad at him. Augusta is the type to let bygones be bygones. Plus, why would she kidnap your father, Nancy? That's just crazy."

"Then explain why her manuscript was at Dr. Burnham's house," Bess said.

"I bet he sneaked a copy of it from one of his colleagues who used to teach her. She often solicits advice from her former teachers. Dr. Burnham probably felt paranoid and wanted to make sure she wasn't plagiarizing him again. So he somehow got hold of a copy."

"How do you explain the note that led me to Todd?" I asked. "Augusta was with us when I got it. She could have bribed the waiter to plant it on my plate."

Duncan shot me a skeptical look. "Even if she had the opportunity to plant it, why would she lead you to Todd?"

"Well, someone did," Bess said firmly.

"Not Augusta," Duncan retorted. "Anyway, girls, we have to end this talk. I'm due back onstage. I guess I can understand why you were spying on me. You're under a lot of pressure, and I suppose I can forgive your ridiculous accusations. But I can tell you right now—I'm innocent and so is Augusta. So I don't want to catch you snooping around us anymore."

"We won't," I promised, though I knew I'd be back if his story didn't check out. "And please let us know if you find out where Todd's parents are." Jotting down the phone number of the White Swan Hotel on some scrap paper, I handed it to Duncan.

"No problem," Duncan said affably as he opened the dressing-room door. As Bess and I slipped through the backstage entrance, a young man who was waiting there grinned at Duncan.

"Xavier?" I murmured to Bess as we left the theater.

Once outside, in the crowd of standing onlookers, I whispered to Bess that I was leaving to search for Todd. "But you don't have to come with me," I added. "You're enjoying the show."

"Of course I'll come, Nancy!" Bess declared. "I wouldn't enjoy it anyway knowing that you might need my help."

Twenty minutes later Bess and I stepped out of a cab on a street corner near Todd. Once inside, we met the owner herself, a stylish woman in her twenties with long dark hair. Her rosy cheeks against her pale delicate complexion reminded me of Snow White. After we introduced ourselves, I said, "Bess and I were browsing at your store last night, chatting with your friend, Duncan Smithson. Did he come into work this morning, by any chance?"

"Oh yes," Todd said, smiling. "Duncan was here all morning helping me."

So his alibi stood up. I briefed Todd on the burglary at Dr. Burnham's house, then added, "This is a very awkward thing to mention, but your parents are the prime suspects in the burglary. Do you have any idea where they are?"

Todd looked unsettled. "I haven't seen my dad in years, though Mum sometimes drops by the store to say hi. Unfortunately, Nancy, my parents are crooks, but they're cagey enough to stay one step ahead of the law. I don't want any part of them. I feel awful admitting that, but I've worked hard to build a productive life for myself and I don't want it ruined by their crimes."

"I understand your dad had a regular job at the British Museum as a guard," I said. "He must have been honest at one point."

"He was fired from that job when his boss suspected him of stealing, even though no one ever proved it," she explained.

"Bess was attacked at the museum today," I said,

"and one of the guards described a man, who looked like Duncan, running away."

Todd's green eyes flashed. "Duncan is innocent! I bet Dad bribed one of his old friends to lie. My parents haven't liked Duncan ever since he caught Mum stealing an American customer's wallet here at the store."

I gaped at her. I couldn't believe that her parents were such awful criminals. Especially because Todd seemed so law abiding and normal. What had her childhood been like with them? My heart went out to her. Her story made me especially appreciate my own dad, our solid home life, and the support he's always given me.

The next question had to be asked. "Todd, my father was kidnapped two nights ago. Do you think your parents could have anything to do with that?"

Todd's jaw dropped. "I really doubt they'd be that bad, Nancy. I mean, petty thievery is more their style. But they have a perfect place to hide him if they are guilty—a cottage near Stonehenge."

"The police have it covered," Bess said.

Todd frowned. "But there's a fishing shack on the property, hidden in the woods near a stream." She checked her watch. "If you borrow my car, you girls can get to Stonehenge before midnight. The full moon will light your way. How about it?"

13

A Moonlit Stalker

Armed with car keys, take-out dinners, and explicit directions, Bess and I wound our way out of London in the fading spring light. With Bess at the wheel, I knew we'd get there fast. Her expertise with cars and machines includes her driving ability, and she never lets me forget how spacey I can be with stuff like losing car keys and forgetting gas levels. And getting used to driving on the left side of the road.

The suburbs of London soon gave way to a rolling countryside of soft hills that folded into valleys and rose again into more hills. Flowering trees appeared like tiny patches of mist against the dark green forests.

In the passenger's seat, I clenched my fists impatiently as I thought about Dad. Would we find him in the Elliotts' shack? It was awesome to think we might see him in only a couple of hours. Still, even that seemed too long a time for me. And what if he wasn't there?

I couldn't think of that. To distract myself, I talked to Bess about the case so far. "Todd's story supports Duncan's alibi," I said, "which means the museum security guard was either lying or there's another person involved and he looks like Duncan."

"I bet Todd is right," Bess said, as she took a hairpin turn practically on two wheels. "That Mr. Elliott bribed an old friend of his to frame Duncan. But I wonder what that note under your scone was all about? If Duncan and Augusta are innocent, then the Elliotts must have put it there. But why?"

"Maybe to make us suspect Duncan and lead us on a wild-goose chase to distract me from finding clues about Dad and Dr. Burnham."

"What about that voice at the Tower?" Bess asked. "It was definitely a woman, and Augusta was right there."

"It could have been Mrs. Elliott. That place was so crowded, and Mrs. Elliott could have been following us, trying to get us off Dad's track. I saw her so quickly at Dr. Burnham's house—I can't be sure I'd spot her in a big crowd. She might know I'm a detective; maybe she was worried I'd figure things out."

We were silent for a moment, and my mind switched to Dr. Burnham. "Bess, don't you think it's strange that Dr. Burnham's rare copy of *King Lear* was locked in that drawer? If it's so precious, wouldn't he know exactly where it was? He wouldn't have thought it was in the living room when it was in his bedroom all along."

"I still think that maybe it was a different *King Lear*. Not so rare," Bess said.

"Or maybe he's just a typical absentminded professor. But isn't it a little odd that he would have sneaked a copy of Augusta's manuscript to check it for plagiarism? Of course, Duncan was only guessing about that."

"Dr. Burnham's actions haven't always made sense," Bess said, "but how could he be guilty of anything when he's been in America this whole time?"

"And even if he had been around, what would his motive be for kidnapping Dad and stealing his own stuff?" I couldn't wait for Dr. Burnham to arrive so I could ask him why *King Lear* was locked up in his drawer and what Augusta's manuscript had been doing under his sideboard. Right now, I figured, he was probably at the airport waiting to board his plane.

"Anyway," Bess went on, breaking into my thoughts, "the Elliotts are obviously sleazy. It's pretty clear they stole Dr. Burnham's furniture and probably kidnapped your dad."

I sighed. "The question is, why Dad?"

I stuck my hand out the window to feel the air. The evening breeze was warm, and fireflies blew around us like wayward embers. Wherever Dad was, he must be feeling incredibly lonely, but I knew he'd realize that I'd never, never give up searching for him. And that no matter where he was, I'd find him.

Another hour passed, and we suddenly found ourselves zipping along a narrow road beside gently rolling moors. The full moon shone down, bathing the heath in a pearly glow. Suddenly, on a distant hill, a huge circle of enormous rectangular stones rose in the moonlight, making an eerie etching across the sky.

"Look, Bess!" I said, pointing out my window. "Stonehenge."

Bess stole a look from the driver's seat and gaped at the spectacle. "That's one of the coolest sights I think I've ever seen! How old do you think it is?"

"Careful, Bess, keep the car on the road!" I warned as we scraped a roadside hedge. "Anyway, I read somewhere that Stonehenge is around five thousand years old, older than even the Celtic culture in Britain."

"I wonder what it was used for," Bess mused.

"No one really knows why it was built. But it must

have been an awesome job for prehistoric people to move those giant stones. I mean, they've got to weigh tons!"

"The whole place looks so mysterious in the moonlight," Bess said, marveling. "Hey, Nancy, maybe you can solve another mystery once you find your dad."

"Like, who made Stonehenge?" I said, smiling. "Bess, if I find Dad and figure out where Dr. Burnham's stuff is, I'll be totally happy. The Stonehenge mystery can wait for another vacation."

Todd had told us to head right, into a narrow driveway marked by a red mailbox a couple of miles past Stonehenge. As Bess made the turn, we came face-to-face with a ramshackle stone cottage covered with thick roses and a police car parked by the front path.

The house was dark, but a light was on inside the police car, which had its windows rolled down to let in some air. Bess and I got out of Todd's car and approached the young woman in the driver's seat who was reading a book while her partner dozed in the seat next to her.

"Hello!" I said to her. "I'm Nancy Drew."

The policewoman whipped around to face us, tossing down her book. But she relaxed as her gray eyes took us in. "You girls gave me a bit of a start. So you're Nancy Drew. Carson's daughter, I assume?"

I smiled. "Yes. I hope you don't mind if we do some investigating here on our own. I couldn't face sitting in our hotel room while Dad is gone."

The constable gestured grandly. "Be my guest, Nancy. I don't blame you for wanting to check every nook and cranny of the property. I did my best to investigate the cottage and grounds, but if my dad were missing, I'd want to be making an extra effort of my own."

After thanking her, Bess and I headed toward a patch of woods below the cottage. Once there, we followed an overgrown trail, barely visible, to a stream. Todd had told us that the shack was about two hundred yards away from the path, due west of a giant willow near the stream. "I'm so worried we won't find Dad," I murmured as we walked along.

"We'll find him, Nancy. I know it," Bess declared.

With the moon lighting our way and sticks crackling underfoot, we trudged through thick underbrush. The noise was like minifirecrackers exploding in the silent forest.

My ears pricked up, straining to listen. Maybe my imagination was playing tricks on me, but . . . A chill ran through me. Something was off. Some sound. Were there more than two sets of feet that I was hearing?

"Bess!" I whispered, grabbing her arm as we came to a clearing. "Listen!" Leaves crunched. Silence. "Someone else is in the forest."

A shadow loomed ahead of us, silhouetted against the sky like a tree come to life. But it was no tree. It was a man holding a knife. Across the face of the full moon, the knife cut a thin black wedge.

"Nancy Drew," the man said. It was the voice of Dr. Burnham.

14

A Rare Conspiracy

Run, Bess!" I cried, grabbing her arm. "Back to the police."

Bess needed no persuading. We took off the way we'd come, careening around curves in the trail, crunching sticks and leaves underfoot as we ran. My ears absorbed the terrifying sound of Dr. Burnham's hoarse breathing that grew louder and louder as he sprinted behind us, hot on our heels.

"Nancy, stop!" he shouted.

For a kidnapper brandishing a knife on a lonely forest path? Last time I checked, I didn't solve my cases by believing the criminals I busted.

"Nancy, I promise I won't hurt you," Dr. Burnham cried. "Please don't run away from me. We need to talk."

Why waste my breath by answering him? And judging by the sound of Bess's ragged gasps beside me, we both needed every ounce of energy we could summon to stay ahead.

My lungs felt as if they were bursting. Did these woods ever end? I hoped we hadn't strayed from the right trail. I could vaguely see the path ahead of us, but what if we'd veered off from the way back to the cottage?

A crash reverberated through the trees behind us. Without losing speed, I sneaked a look. By the base of a fallen tree a dark motionless heap slumped like a sack of old laundry. Dr. Burnham was down!

I stopped. "Bess, he's not moving. Maybe he's been injured."

Alongside me, Bess said, "Good! I'm about to collapse. Leave the marathon running to George!"

"If Dr. Burnham is hurt, that means we can look for Dad without worrying about being chased. Come on. Let's check him out."

"Watch out, Nancy. He might be pretending."

Bess and I moved hesitantly back toward Dr. Burnham, ready to run at his slightest move. But he remained on the ground as we peered at him from about six feet away. Had he been hurt? I hoped so. I don't mean to seem harsh, but his presence was keeping me from finding Dad.

132

Groaning, Dr. Burnham clutched his ankle. Bess and I circled around him, heading west toward the stream. Bess asked, "Are you sure you don't want to alert that policewoman, Nancy?"

Already I'd forgotten about the cops. Why take up time when Dad might be in danger? Every moment counted. "I want to see if Dad is here, Bess. It's been two days since I've seen him, and I don't want to waste another minute."

We hurried along, careful to keep on the path as the moon lit our way. My ears were on alert for the sound of crackling sticks behind us.

As we rounded a curve, a dark rectangular form appeared in front of us. "What's that?" Bess asked.

"The fishing shack, maybe?"

"It looks like a tool shed," Bess breathed, sounding reassured.

Running the last twenty yards to the shack, I yanked open the door. It almost fell onto me as the rotted wood at the hinges easily gave way.

I peeked inside, holding my breath in suspense. If Dad wasn't there, I'd be back to square one. I couldn't allow that possibility to enter my mind. Squinting through the pitch-black interior, I struggled to make out shapes, but nothing took form. Until the moon crept out from behind a tree and lit up the murky depths.

A shiver went through me. Hunched in a corner, bound and gagged, was Dad!

"Dad!" I cried. His head tilted toward me. Though hidden by the dimness, I knew his eyes would be filled with love and pride. "Dad, it's me, I'm so glad to see you!"

Bess and I hurried to untie him, our fingers working fast. Once free, Dad said hoarsely, "Nancy dear, I knew you'd come!" Then he clasped me in a gigantic hug and Bess in a smaller one. Thank goodness he still had some strength.

"Dad, are you okay?" I asked. Now that I was close to him, I could see his face clearly. Big circles smudged his eyes, and his lips had been chapped by the gag. But he looked alert as he answered, "I'm fine, Nancy. I can't tell you how happy I am to see you girls."

Once he learned that we were okay too, I explained that we were being chased by Dr. Burnham. "We'd better make a run for it. He's going to get here ASAP. Dad, can you walk?"

"I can run!" Dad said gamely. "All I needed was the chance to prove it." Grabbing the rope that had bound him from where it lay on the floor, he added, "I'm putting this in my pocket. It might come in handy in case we catch Dr. Burnham."

We hurried out of the shack, eager to return to

the cottage and the police. "Speaking of Dr. Burnham, he might be on the trail. Maybe we shouldn't retrace our steps," I suggested.

Scanning the hill to our left, I noticed an interruption in the line of trees at the crest. "Maybe from up there, we'll be able to see where the cottage is."

"Okay, Nancy, lead on," Dad said.

The three of us scrabbled to the hilltop. Miles of heathery moorland stretched in front of us. Across the way, Stonehenge rose up, majestic against the silvery sky. To our right the Elliotts' cottage nestled in a dip of the hills.

A rustling noise broke the silence. We whirled around to see a dark figure emerging from the woods below us. Dr. Burnham, blocking our way to the cottage! "Dad, Bess, run!" I shouted as Dr. Burnham headed toward us. "To Stonehenge. It's our only choice."

We raced across the moor, with Dr. Burnham sprinting behind us. The stone monoliths loomed over us as we came closer, offering shelter in their huge dark shadows. Luckily, we found a gap in the chain-link fence surrounding Stonehenge, and the three of us quickly slipped through it. "Over here!" I cried, heading for one of the giant upright stones. "Get behind this one."

Dad, Bess, and I dove behind the stone just as Dr. Burnham dashed by us.

"Phew!" Bess whispered.

I crossed my fingers, hoping we could overpower Dr. Burnham in a sneak attack. His shadow rose against a nearby rock. If only he'd come closer so we could jump him.

In tiny whispers, we plotted our strategy. "Let him make all the moves," I suggested. "We can wait him out."

"Don't move a muscle, girls," Dad said, "or we'll blow our cover."

"So do you think he'll get bored and just go away?" Bess asked.

"He won't give up till he finds us," I said grimly. "Our only option is to ambush him and try to tie him up. At least it's three against one."

"Remember, he's got a weapon," Dad warned.

A minute later we got our chance. Dr. Burnham slipped in front of our boulder, scanning it for signs of his prey. I whispered, "Now!"

We sprang out at him, tackling him by surprise. Offering no resistance, he collapsed to the ground.

"What?" he cried. Then the rest of his words were muffled as Dad's hand clamped across his mouth.

"Here, Nancy, catch," Dad said, throwing me the

rope he'd saved. As Dad and Bess held Dr. Burnham down, I tied up his wrists and ankles.

"Let me go!" Dr. Burnham said as he rolled from side to side, trying his best to escape. "I'm harmless. I wouldn't have hurt you girls for anything."

"Harmless? You threatened us with a knife," I said.

"I thought you were wild animals," he explained. "They exist in these woods, you know."

"If you didn't want to hurt us, then why were you chasing us?" Bess asked. "Plus, the way you treated Mr. Drew wasn't so harmless."

"That's another story!" Dr. Burnham snapped. "The reason I chased you was to ask you not to go to the police. I want you to hear my side of the story first."

"Okay, Dr. Burnham," I said, "but your story had better be good."

He looked at me meekly from where he lay. "The ground is cold and damp," he complained. "Won't you let me sit up while I speak?"

Dad propped him against the stone we'd hidden behind. Once Dr. Burnham was settled, I said, "Tell us why you kidnapped my father."

A stricken look flashed across his eyes. "I'm innocent, Nancy," he said firmly. "I didn't kidnap your father. Just hear me out before you jump to conclusions. You see, I caught an earlier flight to the U.K.

than the one I'd originally booked. Luckily, space became available at the last minute. The instant I landed, I headed here to look for the Elliotts." Anger crossed his face as he added, "Thieves! I know they stole my stuff."

I turned to Dad. "Obviously he meant to hurt you. Otherwise he wouldn't have had a knife. And he meant to hurt us, too. But it's true that he couldn't have kidnapped you, because you'd already disappeared before he left America. So who did?"

"I know exactly who my kidnapper was," Dad said. "The man who slammed the door in our faces at Dr. Burnham's house."

"Mr. Elliott!" I exclaimed. "The Elliotts were my main suspects all along, until we ran into Dr. Burnham tonight."

"I'm not guilty," Dr. Burnham insisted. "The Elliotts are. I'm glad your father is clearing my name. Please untie me, Nancy, so we can join forces and look for those thieves."

"Not so fast, Dr. Burnham," I said. "What makes you think the Elliotts took your furniture?"

"You yourself said they were in the house shortly before my things disappeared," Dr. Burnham sputtered, throwing me a peevish look. "You're a witness, Nancy. Anyway, I'm anxious to find my stuff, especially my copy of *King Lear*. Fortunately, it's heavily insured, but no amount of cash can make up for the real thing. Please untie me. I'm innocent."

I remembered the edition of *King Lear* inside his locked drawer. "What does your copy of *King Lear* look like?" I asked.

His eyes lit up, as if I'd asked him to describe a person he adored. "Oh, what a treasure that book is! So well-cared for! Before I left for America, I oiled the leather so it wouldn't crack. But you asked me what it looks like? Well, it's bound in rich red leather, with gold lettering on it. The binding was put on in the nineteenth century, but I love it even though it's not part of the original."

"What does the title page look like?"

"It announces the history of King Lear and his three daughters. It's a second quarto edition, very rare, dated 1608," he said fondly.

"Well, Dr. Burnham, you're in luck," I announced. "That book wasn't stolen with the rest of your stuff. It's locked safely in your bedside table drawer."

"What? But that's impossible, Nancy!" he said, his meek expression suddenly turning fierce. He strained at his ropes, struggling to get loose. "Why were you snooping in my house?"

"Snooping? Let me refresh your memory, Dr. Burnham. You asked me to investigate the burglary. Of course I was going to look for every possible clue, including ones that might be hidden in locked drawers! Anyway, if you care so much about that book, why aren't you happy that it wasn't stolen?"

Dr. Burnham opened his mouth to reply, then quickly clamped it shut. Once more he fought against the ropes that held him, in a fruitless effort to get free. But my knots were too strong for him. Giving up, Dr. Burnham slumped forward.

And then he straightened, fixing me with a sly sidelong gaze. I'd seen that look before, and I didn't trust it. "I'm glad you found my book, Nancy. Thrilled, in fact," Dr. Burnham purred. "Thank you so much. Now let me go."

"Not until you level with me. Even if you didn't actually take Dad, you're guilty of something. Maybe you hired Mr. Elliott to kidnap him, and I'd like to know why."

"I did nothing of the sort!" Dr. Burnham protested.

"Then tell me the truth," I pressed. My mind clicked onto something he'd mentioned—that his book was heavily insured. "Dr. Burnham, I'm beginning to understand. You planned the theft of your furniture and books to get insurance money!"

His eyes snapped with anger. I went on, "You might as well admit it. If you're cooperative, I'm sure you'll receive a lighter sentence."

Dr. Burnham sighed, as if he was a balloon slowly deflating. "Okay, Nancy," he said in a resigned tone. "You're right. I staged the theft of my living room to disguise the disappearance of my rare edition of *King Lear* so that I could get the insurance money. My furniture is in a London storage unit, but I locked the book away in a place I thought was secure before I left London. Obviously I wasn't careful enough."

"And you hired the Elliotts to help you, I guess?" I prompted.

Dr. Burnham nodded. "I needed the money desperately, Nancy. I had my sights on a rare edition of *Macbeth* that I'd seen at a store called Books of Olde, but I didn't want to sell my edition of *King Lear*, which I dearly love, to finance the purchase. So I concocted this scheme. I scraped together enough money for Elliott to reserve the *Macbeth* edition for me. Once I got my insurance money, I'd have enough to pay the balance to the store."

"He must have dropped the address of Books of Olde on Dad's floor by mistake then," I said, musing. "By the way, I don't think Mr. Elliott reserved *Macbeth*, because when I stopped by the store yesterday, it was still available."

"That worm!" Dr. Burnham cried. "He must have run off with my money." He paused, then added, "Nancy, I promise I never kidnapped Mr. Drew—or

141

arranged to have him kidnapped. I'm innocent of that, I tell you!"

"Then why did Mr. Elliott take my father?" Turning to Dad, I asked, "Do you know why he kidnapped you, Dad?"

"No idea," Dad said. "When I returned to my hotel room after leaving you girls, I discovered Mr. Elliott going through my stuff. Before I was able to call for help, he clamped his hand over my mouth. The next thing I knew, I woke up in the back of a speeding car, bound and gagged, with an awful headache. Once we arrived here, he marched me into the shack. Other than taking off my gag when he brought me meals, he completely ignored me."

"But why did Mr. Elliott go into your room in the first place?" I wondered.

"I can answer that," Dr. Burnham cut in. "Mr. Drew, Elliott noticed that you bore a resemblance to him the instant he saw you at my door. So he quickly sneaked off to your room, hoping you'd left your passport there so he could steal it and come to America. When you surprised him, he didn't want you to rat on him, so he knocked you out and brought you to his cottage. So you see, I might be guilty of insurance fraud, but I'm innocent of kidnapping."

"How do you know all this?" I asked him.

"I kept in close touch with the Elliotts after they

managed the burglary," Dr. Burnham confessed. "Mr. Elliott told me what was happening, including the abduction of Mr. Drew."

"So why didn't you tell me or the police where Dad was?" I asked. "You may not have deliberately taken him, but you helped cover up the crime."

Dr. Burnham looked stricken. "But if I'd told on Elliott, he would have reported my insurance scheme."

"So you cared more about getting your book than about my father," I said.

"I never said that!" Dr. Burnham snapped. "In fact, the moment Elliott told me about the kidnapping, I came down here to release your father. I brought a ski mask in my pocket so he wouldn't recognize me. Naturally I didn't want to get caught, but I was very concerned about Mr. Drew. Why else do you think I'm here?"

I said nothing, knowing he'd never admit to being part of Mr. Elliott's crime. Time to steer him onto a different track.

"Do you know what was going on in London, with that note and the attack in the museum and the other stuff?" I asked.

"The Elliotts distracted you girls with false leads while they plotted their getaway," Dr. Burnham explained. "They were especially happy to harass

Duncan Smithson by making him a suspect. You see, he'd caught Mrs. Elliott attempting to steal a customer's wallet at her daughter's store last week, which included an American passport that would have been a perfect match for her."

"Mrs. Elliott must have been in the crowd at the Tower," Bess said. "I guess she tried to spook us. It wasn't Augusta."

"Speaking of Augusta, what was her manuscript doing in your house?" I asked Dr. Burnham.

"She steals ideas from me!" Dr. Burnham said fiercely. "I sneaked a copy of Augusta's new play from a friend of mine she'd given it to. I had to make sure she wasn't plagiarizing my work again."

"And what about the attack at the British Museum?" I asked. "What was that all about?"

Dr. Burnham shrugged. "I had nothing to do with that, Nancy. Elliott was probably responsible. He told me he was doing his best to scare you and distract you, so you wouldn't find out what was going on. He was worried that you would find out the truth."

"Mr. Elliott probably attacked me and bribed one of his friends to blame it on Duncan," Bess said.

"Whatever," Dr. Burnham said blithely. "The bottom line is, I'm innocent. I didn't kidnap Mr. Drew, I attacked no one, and I haven't even committed insurance fraud since I haven't had a chance to file a claim yet. You have nothing to hang on me, Nancy."

"What I don't get is why you wanted me to check your house in the first place?" I asked. "Why bother to give me a key that didn't work?"

"I wanted you to witness the timing of the theft so no one would suspect me," he replied. "You knew I was in America while my house was being robbed. I just didn't reckon on your determination, Nancy, especially when someone you love is in danger!"

Two figures appeared on the horizon behind us. "Is everything okay here?" a woman's voice asked. As they came closer, I recognized the policewoman who'd been staking out the Elliotts' cottage with her partner.

After I gave the police a rundown on everything that had happened since we'd seen them an hour ago, they immediately radioed for backup. They also alerted Constable Reynolds, who issued an all points bulletin for the Elliotts at borders in the U.K. "Don't worry, Ms. Drew," the policewoman assured me, smiling, "we'll find Mr. and Mrs. Elliott. They'll be brought in on kidnapping charges, and our friend Dr. Burnham here will be prosecuted for conspiring to commit insurance fraud. Maybe he thinks he can get off, but he won't, I promise."

As for Dad, Bess, and me, we eagerly resumed our

lives as American tourists in London. Driving back that night in Todd's car, Bess said, "So what shall we visit tomorrow, everyone? The Sherlock Holmes Museum? Abbey Road Studios? Parliament?"

"Anything you girls want to do is fine by me," Dad said, stretching his legs in the front seat next to Bess. "I'm just glad to be out of that fishing shack."

"Me too," I said, shooting him a relieved smile. "Dad, you're the greatest. That's why this case was so hard. It was *you* in jeopardy this time."

He grinned, his blue eyes sparkling. "Nancy, I knew you'd fix that soon enough. I had total confidence in you. And see? I was right!"

The road back to London wound through the countryside, which looked cool and mysterious in the moonlight. While Dad nodded off, I felt even more awake. Out there was a whole world of mysteries waiting to be discovered. I was so thankful I'd solved this one, and who knew? Maybe I'd even get a few days to relax before the next one came my way.

Think it would be fun to get stuck on a deserted island with the guy you sort of like? Well, try adding the girl who gets on your nerves big-time (*and* who's crushing on the same guy), the bossiest kid in school, your annoying little brother, and a bunch of other people, all of whom have their own ideas about how things should be done. Oh, and have I mentioned that there's no way off this island, and no one knows where you are?

Still sound great? Didn't think so.

Now all I have to worry about is getting elected island leader, finding something to wear for a dance (if you can believe that), and surviving a hurricane, all while keeping my crush away from Little Miss Priss. Oh, and one other teeny-tiny little thing: surviving.

Get me outta here!

Read all the books in the Castaways trilogy:

#1 Worst Class Trip Ever

#2 Weather's Here, Wish You Were Great

#3 Isle Be Seeing You

REDISCOVER THE CLASSIC MYSTERIES OF NANCY DREW

____ Nancy Drew #1:
The Secret of the Old Clock
____ Nancy Drew #2:
The Hidden Staircase
____ Nancy Drew #3:
The Bungalow Mystery
____ Nancy Drew #4:
The Mystery at Lilac Inn
____ Nancy Drew #5:
The Secret of Shadow Ranch
____ Nancy Drew #6:
The Secret of Red Gate Farm
____ Nancy Drew #7:
The Clue in the Diary
____ Nancy Drew #8:
Nancy's Mysterious Letter
____ Nancy Drew #9:
The Sign of the Twisted Candles
____ Nancy Drew #10:
Password to Larkspur Lane
____ Nancy Drew #11:
The Clue of the Broken Locket
____ Nancy Drew #12:
The Message in the Hollow Oak
____ Nancy Drew #13:
The Mystery of the Ivory Charm
____ Nancy Drew #14:
The Whispering Statue
____ Nancy Drew #15:
The Haunted Bridge
____ Nancy Drew #16:
The Clue of the Tapping Heels
____ Nancy Drew #17: *The Mystery of the Brass-Bound Trunk*
____ Nancy Drew #18: *The Mystery of the Moss-Covered Mansion*
____ Nancy Drew #19:
The Quest of the Missing Map
____ Nancy Drew #20:
The Clue in the Jewel Box
____ Nancy Drew #21:
The Secret in the Old Attic
____ Nancy Drew #22:
The Clue in the Crumbling Wall
____ Nancy Drew #23:
The Mystery of the Tolling Bell
____ Nancy Drew #24:
The Clue in the Old Album
____ Nancy Drew #25:
The Ghost of Blackwood Hall
____ Nancy Drew #26:
The Clue of the Leaning Chimney
____ Nancy Drew #27:
The Secret of the Wooden Lady
____ Nancy Drew #28:
The Clue of the Black Keys
____ Nancy Drew #29:
Mystery at the Ski Jump

____ Nancy Drew #30:
The Clue of the Velvet Mask
____ Nancy Drew #31:
The Ringmaster's Secret
____ Nancy Drew #32:
The Scarlet Slipper Mystery
____ Nancy Drew #33:
The Witch Tree Symbol
____ Nancy Drew #34:
The Hidden Window Mystery
____ Nancy Drew #35:
The Haunted Showboat
____ Nancy Drew #36:
The Secret of the Golden Pavilion
____ Nancy Drew #37:
The Clue in the Old Stagecoach
____ Nancy Drew #38:
The Mystery of the Fire Dragon
____ Nancy Drew #39:
The Clue of the Dancing Puppet
____ Nancy Drew #40:
The Moonstone Castle Mystery
____ Nancy Drew #41:
The Clue of the Whistling Bagpipes
____ Nancy Drew #42:
The Phantom of Pine Hill
____ Nancy Drew #43:
The Mystery of the 99 Steps
____ Nancy Drew #44:
The Clue in the Crossword Cipher
____ Nancy Drew #45:
The Spider Sapphire Mystery
____ Nancy Drew #46:
The Invisible Intruder
____ Nancy Drew #47:
The Mysterious Mannequin
____ Nancy Drew #48:
The Crooked Banister
____ Nancy Drew #49:
The Secret of Mirror Bay
____ Nancy Drew #50:
The Double Jinx Mystery
____ Nancy Drew #51:
The Mystery of the Glowing Eye
____ Nancy Drew #52:
The Secret of the Forgotten City
____ Nancy Drew #53:
The Sky Phantom
____ Nancy Drew #54: *The Strange Message in the Parchment*
____ Nancy Drew #55:
Mystery of Crocodile Island
____ Nancy Drew #56:
The Thirteenth Pearl
Nancy Drew Mystery Stories

star power

by Catherine Hapka

She's beautiful, she's talented, she's famous.

She's a star!

Things would be perfect
if only her family
was around to help
her celebrate. . . .

Follow the
adventures of
fourteen-year-old
pop star
Star Calloway